✓ 7/16

Praise for tl

**LOWCOU**

MW01025903

"The authentically Southern boyer writes with heart, insight, and a deep understanding of human nature."

– Hank Phillippi Ryan,
Agatha Award-Winning Author of *What You See*

"An exciting, humorous mystery...authentically Southern. I absolutely love reading about my hometown and have been known to go check out a location to see if she got it right—she always does!"

– Martha Thomas Rudisill,
Artist and 11th Generation Charlestonian

"Southern family eccentricities and manners, a very strongly plotted mystery, and a heroine who must balance her nuptials with a murder investigation ensure that readers will be vastly entertained by this funny and compelling mystery."

– *Kings River Life Magazine*

**LOWCOUNTRY BONEYARD (#3)**

"Has everything you could want in a traditional mystery...I enjoyed every minute of it."

– Charlaine Harris,
*New York Times* Bestselling Author of *Day Shift*

"Like the other Lowcountry mysteries, there's tons of humor here, but in *Lowcountry Boneyard* there's a dash of darkness, too. A fun and surprisingly thought-provoking read."

– *Mystery Scene Magazine*

"The local foods sound scrumptious and the locale descriptions entice us to be tourists...the PI detail is as convincing as Grafton."

– *Fresh Fiction*

## LOWCOUNTRY BOMBSHELL (#2)

"Boyer delivers big time with a witty mystery that is fun, radiant, and impossible to put down. I love this book!"

– Darynda Jones,
*New York Times* Bestselling Author

"*Lowcountry Bombshell* is that rare combination of suspense, humor, seduction, and mayhem, an absolute must-read not only for mystery enthusiasts but for anyone who loves a fast-paced, well-written story."

– Cassandra King,
Author of *The Same Sweet Girls* and *Moonrise*

"A complicated story that's rich and juicy with plenty of twists and turns. It has lots of peril and romance—something for every cozy mystery fan."

– *New York Journal of Books*

## LOWCOUNTRY BOIL (#1)

"Imaginative, empathetic, genuine, and fun, *Lowcountry Boil* is a lowcountry delight."

– Carolyn Hart,
Author of *What the Cat Saw*

"*Lowcountry Boil* pulls the reader in like the draw of a riptide with a keeps-you-guessing mystery full of romance, family intrigue, and the smell of salt marsh on the Charleston coast."

– Cathy Pickens,
Author of the *Southern Fried Mysteries* and *Charleston Mysteries*

"Plenty of secrets, long-simmering feuds, and greedy ventures make for a captivating read...Boyer's chick lit PI debut charmingly showcases South Carolina island culture."

– *Library Journal*

# Lowcountry
# BOOK CLUB

**The Liz Talbot Mystery Series
by Susan M. Boyer**

LOWCOUNTRY BOIL (#1)

LOWCOUNTRY BOMBSHELL (#2)

LOWCOUNTRY BONEYARD (#3)

LOWCOUNTRY BORDELLO (#4)

LOWCOUNTRY BOOK CLUB (#5)

# Lowcountry
# BOOK CLUB

### A Liz Talbot Mystery

## Susan M. Boyer

HENERY PRESS

LOWCOUNTRY BOOK CLUB
A Liz Talbot Mystery
Part of the Henery Press Mystery Collection

First Edition | July 2016

Henery Press
www.henerypress.com

Trade Paperback ISBN-13: 978-1-63511-045-6
Digital epub ISBN-13: 978-1-63511-046-3
Kindle ISBN-13: 978-1-63511-047-0
Hardcover Paperback ISBN-13: 978-1-63511-048-7

Printed in the United States of America

*For my daughter,*
*(picky people will want to add the word 'step' in there,*
*but I never do)*
*Jennifer Elaine Boyer Teague,*
*with much love*
*and with gratitude for all the things you've taught me.*
*One of the more memorable is that I should make Dad*
*a tomato sandwich with a lot of mayonnaise for dinner*
*so I can get to my workout.*

# ACKNOWLEDGMENTS

Heartfelt thanks to...

...each and every reader—you make my life possible.

...booksellers, you are rock stars. To those of you who stock the Liz Talbot Mysteries and recommend them to your customers, I am forever in your debt.

...Jim Boyer, my wonderful husband, best friend, and fiercest advocate, thank you could never cover it, nevertheless, thank you for everything you do to help me live my dream.

...everyone at Henery Press—Kendel Lynn, Art Molinares, Erin George, and Rachel Jackson, this book is better because of all of you. Thank you for all you do. I count myself as very fortunate to be a Henery Press author.

...Mary Alice Monroe for the lovely cover blurb for this book. I'm delighted beyond measure.

...my dear friends Martha and Mary Rudisill, eleventh and twelfth-generation Charlestonians, respectively, thank you for your continued enthusiastic assistance.

...Gretchen Smith, my dear friend and partner in a great many shenanigans—you know what you did.

...the word's best sister, Sabrina Niggle, who finds my mistakes when I can no longer see them.

...the world's best mom, and very likely the world's most voracious reader, Claudette Jones.

...my dear friend Marcia Migacz, who I swear has eagle eyes.

...Amy Wilson, Vice President, Development at One8oPlace, for her input. I'm in awe of the work they do on behalf of those in need.

Special thanks to the 'guest stars' in this book. Angela McConnell and Mary Bernard won appearances through generous contributions to charities near and dear to my heart, Ada Jenkins Center and Greenville Literacy Association, respectively. Also appearing is Mariel Camp, who was the first member of a book club I visited to suggest *Lowcountry Book Club* as a title. Additional guest stars are the remaining members of Books & Wine with Wendi, a local book club that always welcomes me. Its members are enthusiastic supporters of Liz Talbot: Liz Bell, Erin Guidici, Anne Spence, Nerissa (whose last name isn't Long) and a return engagement from Heather Wilder who wants to marry Blake Talbot. None of these guest stars are anything like the characters in the book.

As always, unending thanks to Kathie Bennett and Susan Zurenda at Magic Time Literary.

Thank you, Claire McKinney and Larissa Ackerman at ClaireMcKinneyPR. I'm excited about what the future holds.

Thank you always, Jill Hendrix, owner of Fiction Addiction book store, for your ongoing support.

As always, I'm terrified I've forgotten someone. If I have, please know it was unintentional and in part due to sleep deprivation. I am truly grateful to everyone who has helped me along this journey.

# ONE

The dead are not abundantly sympathetic to their own. My best friend, Colleen, passed through the veil and into the great mystery eighteen years ago next month. She shed no tears over Shelby Scott Poinsett Gerhardt.

The photos of Shelby sprawled lifeless as a rag doll in the brick courtyard of her Tradd Street home would haunt me. I passed them to Nate, who was seated on my right in Fraser Rutledge's office. Fraser was the senior partner at Rutledge and Radcliffe, a prestigious Charleston law firm.

"She'll be much happier now." Colleen's tone rang casual to my ear. She should be ashamed of herself.

Colleen read my mind, literally.

"What?" Her jade green eyes telegraphed impatience. "Shelby was taken before her time. She'll be back with a mission soon enough. I hear tell helping others is what this woman lived for. Leaving this life is not the tragedy you mortals think it is. It's true what they say. She's in a better place."

I closed my eyes in an effort to shut her out. She was a distraction in her blue polka dot sundress, a wide-brimmed hat atop her long red curls, perched as she was on the corner of Fraser Alston Rutledge III's heirloom desk. Of course only Nate and I could see or hear her.

Nate cleared his throat, muttered something.

I made out the words "control" and "ghost."

I gave my head a little shake. As if. Nate was still coming to terms with Colleen. Right up until we'd said our "I Dos" in December, he'd been blissfully unaware of her presence in our lives. It was early May, and he still had a ways to go.

"Am I somehow failing to hold your interest?" Fraser elongated each syllable, his honeyed drawl spiked with irritation.

My eyes popped open. I felt at a disadvantage. We sat on the other side of his desk in his elegantly appointed Broad Street law office. Everything about the man and his surroundings, from the oil painting of him with two Brittany spaniels hanging on the cypress-paneled wall, to the black and white striped bowtie he wore with his grey seersucker suit, testified that his bona fides were in order, his Charleston heritage long and storied.

Fraser studied me.

"Quite to the contrary." Nate's easy tone sought to diffuse Fraser's pique. "We'll hold our questions for when you've finished outlining the case against your client. We're eager to help, if we can."

"Please continue," I said.

"You appear somewhat distracted." Fraser looked from me to Nate. "We cannot afford to piss away any more time. Our former investigator twiddled his Johnson for four months, billed us a sultan's ransom, and found not one solitary shred of information we can use. Jury selection begins in two weeks."

I looked past Colleen directly into Fraser's eyes. They were tiger eyes, gold and speckled with brown. "You were telling us about your client."

"Clint Gerhardt." Eli Radcliffe didn't quite spit the name out of his mouth, but he managed to convey his disapproval of Clint Gerhardt and all his ancestors. Eli, Fraser's partner, sat to my left in one of four deep leather visitor chairs. "Naturally, we want to be as prepared as possible."

"He doesn't believe Clint Gerhardt is innocent." Sometimes Colleen could read other minds besides mine. "He's mad as blazes at his partner."

*You think?* I threw the sarcasm-laced thought in her direction. Apparently, the message was also inscribed on my face.

Fraser caught my expression. He drew back, his visage washed in incredulity.

Let him interpret that look however he pleased. I was exhausted from listening to him talk. Why was Eli so mad at Fraser?

"Eli." I rolled my voice in sugar sprinkles. "I'd love to hear your take on the case. Is there an avenue you think we should pursue first?"

From the corner of my eye, I caught Fraser's raised eyebrow. "By all means, Eli. Enlighten them."

Eli inhaled deeply, averted his soft brown eyes.

I scrutinized his profile. Flawless skin, the color of milk chocolate truffles, high cheekbones, and a strong chin made for a noble countenance. They were a study in similarities and contrasts, these three Southern men. All were well-educated, well-groomed, and fit. All spoke the native language of our people, understood the context words carried here. All had lovely drawls. Nate was the blue-eyed, blond-haired, laid-back prototype; Fraser the wealthy, eccentric, Old Charleston model; and Eli the self-made, cautious, black man.

Eli said, "It doesn't matter what I think. Our client is innocent until proven guilty. We need to mount a vigorous defense, with a credible theory of the crime that does not include Clint Gerhardt throwing his wife out the second floor french doors of their home. Confidentially, Mrs. Gerhardt was prone to taking in strays. Most people, certainly the police, think Mr. Gerhardt is one she should've left at the pound."

Fraser slammed his palm on his desk. "*Dammit*, Eli."

Fraser's wild-eyed expression was that of a street-corner preacher with his soul on fire for The Lord. His brown hair, combed back on the sides, sported sufficient gel that every strand on top stood straight up on end, giving him the look of someone who'd suffered a recent electrical shock. The overall effect announced he was a character. But he was an extremely successful character. At forty, Fraser Alston Rutledge III had a winning record that rivaled that of any Charleston attorney.

He stood and went to testifying. "Shelby Poinsett was an angel put on this earth by God Almighty himself. She had a heart as big as the Atlantic. Yes, dammit, she took in strays of all kinds, animals—hell, her house is a damn petting zoo—people...It didn't matter if you were looking up to catch a fading glimmer of rock bottom, Shelby cared about your *po-ten-tial*. When I was a pimply thirteen-year-old geek whose daddy went to prison for securities fraud, Shelby took me under her wing and double-dog dared anyone at Porter-Gaud

Middle to make fun of me. *I*, Eli, am one of Shelby's strays."

Eli's shoulders rose and fell. "Fraser, I'm well aware of your history with the victim and her husband, our client. Which is one of the many reasons I believe taking this case was a mistake."

Eli struck me as one who was careful with his words. He must've wanted this noted on the record between us.

Fraser placed his palms on his desk and leaned across it. Like the best Southern preachers, there was a cadence in his speech as it rose and fell. It was hypnotic, poetic, regardless of the words. "Clint Gerhardt adored his wife. He was as devoted to her as any man who ever walked this earth has ever been to a woman. He would've died protecting her. I am telling you. I *know*. Clint did not kill Shelby. And I will be damned if I sit idly by while he is railroaded to death row because he is from, saints preserve us all, *off*. And because some folks hear the words Army Ranger and are convinced he is a violent man."

Charleston natives often referred to those who'd arrived after birth as being from off. The farther away you came from, the more of your history they'd need to know before they fully accepted you. Unless of course they knew your people.

Eli stared at the wall of bookcases behind Fraser's desk looking like maybe he'd heard this sermon a time or two. He was neither intimidated nor impressed by his partner's theatrics. "Bottom line. The Gerhardts were at home alone on December 28. At approximately nine p.m., Mrs. Gerhardt was pushed from the french doors of the second-floor library. She died of head injuries. Mr. Gerhardt maintains he was in his third-floor study listening to music. He discovered Mrs.

Gerhardt's body when he came downstairs at eleven. He then called 911. Mr. Gerhardt has no knowledge of anyone else being inside the home. Mrs. Gerhardt had no known enemies, and Paul Baker, our erstwhile in-house investigator, uncovered none during his investigation."

Fraser stared at me, taking my measure. "Wally Fayssoux up in Greenville says the two of you are the best investigators in the state. High praise. You have certainly been in the Charleston news of late. However, I remain unconvinced that is an advantage."

Nate leaned back in his chair, likely forming a thoughtful response.

I said, "We've been in the news, Mr. Rutledge, because we solve cases."

"*Miz* Talbot, all due respect, but if I did not know that, we would not be having this conversation."

I resisted the urgent need to liberate him from his burdensomely high self-regard. "The only way being in the news could hamper our effectiveness," I said, "would be if our faces were familiar. You may have noticed how our photographs are missing from the occasional mention in the *Post and Courier*. Very few people in this city could pick us out of a lineup. Why, I'd lay odds you yourself had no idea what we looked like before we walked in."

"As a matter of fact, I did not." Fraser tilted his head in consideration. "All right then. Show me what you can do. Impress me, and this could turn out to be a very lucrative situation for you long term. It will save time if you read through the case file before we get to your questions." He tapped his index finger on the thick stack of documents and photos in the folder lying open in the center of his desk.

"What say we meet again tomorrow morning, ten o'clock." He raised his voice. "Mercedes."

Mercedes glided into the room. Tall and pale with a long neck, her blonde hair, an array of shades similar to mine, was pulled up into a smooth chignon.

Fraser said, "Mercedes, get Mr. Andrews and Miz Talbot a copy of everything we have on Clint and Shelby."

"It's waiting for them out front," she said.

"Why, of course it is," Fraser said. "You keep this place running, don't you, darlin'?" He flipped through the retainer agreement in front of him, initialing where indicated, and then dashed a signature on two copies and handed the documents to Mercedes. "File one of these. The other belongs to our potential investigative team."

Mercedes handed me our copy and was back out the door as we stood.

Fraser watched her go. "She prefers women. Damned unfortunate waste, but it keeps things simple around the office. My wife purely has no patience with me sleeping with the help."

Just then I was thinking how Mrs. Rutledge must have the patience of a saint. My mouth itched to open and opine as much. Nate read my mood, reached out and touched my arm. "It was a pleasure meeting you both." He offered Eli his right hand.

Eli nodded. "I look forward to working with you."

Fraser walked around the side of his desk. He smiled at me with genuine warmth, then took Nate's hand and patted him on the back. "You have got yourself a tiger by the tail, don't you, son?"

"Mr. Rutledge, I don't have a grip at all," said Nate.

On the Broad Street sidewalk, less than a block from East Bay, we turned away from the Old Exchange and headed west. We'd parked on the street between State and Church. Nate and I each carried two file boxes' worth of the Gerhardt case. We'd have to work all night to get through this and be back by ten the next morning. Whatever it took. Fraser's poignant recollections of little Shelby sticking up for him in the schoolyard, coupled with the photographs documenting how her life had been abruptly cut short, had stirred my need to set things right. As right as they could now be set anyway.

Colleen trailed behind us.

Nate said, "Colleen, it's not my intention to sound ungrateful for your help, but there are times when I would be in your debt if you could just stay in the background. Behind me, where I can't see you, would be ideal."

"There's no connection to my mission here," she said. "I'm going to be of limited help. Strictly protection."

Colleen's mission—what she was sent back from beyond to do—is to protect Stella Maris, the barrier island northeast of Charleston, South Carolina, where our hometown by the same name was situated. Stella Maris chiefly required defense from those who would like to line our pristine beaches with hotels, condos, and all manner of commercial enterprise. Since I was on the town council and heavily invested in maintaining the quality of our small-town life, protecting me was part of Colleen's job.

Nate said, "We'll holler if we need you."

"Yeah, try that sometime," I said.

Colleen appeared in front of us, sitting cross-legged on the rich Charleston breeze. "That's not fair. I've always been there when you needed me."

"Yes, you have," I said. "And we're grateful. But you have to admit, you rarely show up if we simply call your name."

"I stay busy," she said. "And I'm not your dog." She disappeared like someone flipped her switch, not her typical fade out.

"She's going to be seventeen forever, you know," I said.

"It's like having a teenager no one else can see. We'll be lucky if we don't both end up in an institution, either because people think we're mad as sunbathing raccoons or she drives us that way."

We reached his brown Ford Explorer, put the boxes in the back, and climbed in. As Nate pulled into Broad Street traffic, I pressed the button to open the moonroof. The sparkling clear Carolina blue sky and warm May air were irresistible.

"What do you think?" I asked.

"About Fraser Rutledge or about the case?"

"The case."

"It's worrisome that Paul Baker couldn't find anything. I don't know him, but I would venture a guess that our new friend Fraser doesn't suffer incompetence. Sounds like Baker worked for Rutledge and Radcliffe a while. He must be a decent investigator." Nate turned left onto East Bay.

"But if he'd found something we wouldn't have this opportunity." Part of our business plan was to develop relationships with Charleston attorneys. We had ties with several firms in Greenville, in the South Carolina Upstate near the Blue Ridge foothills. We'd established Talbot & Andrews there right after we'd finished our internship fourteen years earlier. But we needed to build our Lowcountry clientele. Although we still owned a condo in downtown Greenville, Stella Maris was home.

"Fair point," said Nate. "My concern is what if there's nothing to find? Given Fraser Rutledge's high regard for his client, if we fail him, I don't think we'll get a second chance."

I sighed, looked out the window at palm trees and storefronts passing by. "We can only do our best and pray that if there's something to find, we find it. I can't bear to think he's innocent and there's no way to prove it. That's not the way it's supposed to work."

"If he's innocent, all they have is circumstantial evidence," said Nate. "But those are some hellacious circumstances."

# TWO

It would've been a sinful waste not to have lunch outside on a day as beautiful as that spring Tuesday. Back home on Stella Maris, a twenty-minute ferry ride from the Isle of Palms marina, we toted the legal boxes that made up the Gerhardt file into my office. Then I made chicken salad sandwiches, and we took them out to the Adirondack chairs on the deck overlooking the Atlantic. The rambling yellow beach house my grandmother left me was fringed on all sides by porches, but this was our favorite spot. Rhett, my golden retriever, stretched out in the sun at our feet.

The rhythmic song of waves on the sand worked the tension from me. I inhaled a deep, cleansing breath of salt air. How blessed was I to live in this magical place.

"I appreciate you not putting Fraser Rutledge in his proper place," said Nate. "I was sorely tempted to take care of that bit of business myself, but this case calls to me."

"Me too. But dear Heaven, what nerve that man has. A tiger by the tail. *Miz* Talbot. Clearly he disapproves of me. Proper Southern ladies take their husband's last name. And they most assuredly are not private investigators. Whatever. I want justice for Shelby and Clint. On that we can agree. And Fraser surely is entertaining."

"He is that. And he has three last names. First one's spelled funny."

"Those are all likely family names. I bet his ancestry is fascinating."

"Is this your mamma's chicken salad?"

"I made it. Why?"

"This is the best chicken salad I've ever tasted in my life."

"You like hers better."

"She uses the bad-for-you mayonnaise."

"Get used to it."

"I'm not complaining, Mrs. Andrews. This is fine chicken salad. And I appreciate your care with our health."

"I love it when you call me that." I smiled from the joy of it. "You really do understand, don't you?"

"Why you won't legally take my name? Of course I understand, Slugger. Don't go letting Fraser Rutledge get under your skin."

"I can be your wife without notifying the DMV and ordering new stationery."

"You're a fine wife. Even if you aren't a hundred percent proper. Truth be told, the more improper you are, the better I like it." His slow grin made all manner of suggestions.

A fire ignited deep in my core. I sipped my iced tea, doused the flames as best I could. "We have work to do. How about you start going through those boxes, and I'll start setting up profiles for Shelby, Clint, and anyone with a connection to the case. You can toss me names as you come across them."

"That'll work."

We finished our lunch and headed inside. Rhett snuffed his disapproval and scampered down the steps to play in the yard. Nate and I settled into the large room off the front hall. Originally a living room roughly the size of a ballroom—Gram had loved to entertain—it now served multiple functions. The front half, to the right as you walked in, was still a living room, with an oversized green sofa flanked by wingbacks in a tropical print. Straight ahead, on the far wall, was a fireplace with two reading chairs. The left side of the room held my desk and two leather visitor chairs. Bookcases lined the wall behind my desk and on either side of the fireplace. Though we'd furnished a separate office for Nate in one of the former guest rooms, we most often worked together in here.

"I'm going to set up the case board and grab a couple of six-foot tables to spread this stuff out on," he said.

"Hey, would you hand me Shelby's death certificate from the file?"

"Sure thing." He opened the box marked "1" and flipped through the folders.

I turned on my computer. Nate laid the form on my desk on his way to the storage room underneath the house adjacent to the garage. By the time he came back, I was deep into setting up an electronic case file for Clint Gerhardt. Through Rutledge and Radcliffe, he was our client. But in my mind, the client was his deceased wife, Shelby. I would start with her.

I began my profile with her basic data, which was on her death certificate. I liked to know as much about everyone involved as possible. It was impossible to predict when you started a case what would end up being important. So much information was available online to anyone who cared to look, about any of us. Especially if the person looking had a date of birth to start with. Beyond that, Nate and I had access to several subscription databases which broadened the information we could collect. But the first thing I pulled up was her obituary.

Shelby had been forty years old when she died on December 28. We'd been on our honeymoon when it happened. She was survived by her husband, Clint. They had no children. Her parents, Williams and Tallulah Poinsett, were still living, lifelong Charleston residents. Shelby had one brother, Thomas, who lived in San Francisco with his wife and four children. In lieu of flowers, the family requested memorials to Shelby's favorite charity, One80Place, a local nonprofit organization that managed, among other things, a homeless shelter, a community kitchen, veterans' services, and legal services.

"The Charleston PD detectives assigned to the case were Bissell and Jenkins," said Nate.

"Mmm." I winced. That gave me pause. We'd crossed paths with them a few times. They were good guys. Good detectives. But not infallible, I admonished myself. It was a universal assumption that a dead wife had left behind a guilty husband precisely because that was so often the case. Bissell and Jenkins were following the most common theory of the crime. Given the unique circumstances, they could hardly be faulted. That didn't make them right.

Next I checked the local news coverage of Shelby's death. I scanned for quotes from people who knew her. The staff and board members of One80Place were well represented. Shelby had been a long-time, dedicated volunteer as well as a generous donor. One80Place. That name rang a bell. Didn't they used to be Crisis Ministries? I pulled up the website.

Impressive. The organization featured a long list of

services for those facing dire circumstances, with clear directions to get help. Their mission statement was to provide "food, shelter, and hope to end homelessness and hunger one person at a time, one family at a time." Surely, here were God's angels at work.

They had a staff of more than seventy and a board of directors that listed former Charleston Mayor Joe Riley as Chairman emeritus. I clicked the Google Maps link.

The building was located at the end of Walnut Street, between Meeting and King, on the Upper Peninsula, not far from I-26. Wasn't that near the "tent city" where some homeless folks had been camping on Department of Transportation land? The issue had been in the news a good bit recently. I Googled "Charleston SC Tent City" and pulled up a long list of articles and photos. One of the photos led me to an article in *Charleston City Paper*. I scanned it. In March, some of the campsite residents had moved into One80Place. Others resisted the structured environment of a shelter. A whirlwind of controversy, with high emotions on all sides, surrounded the tent city. Had Shelby somehow become involved in a dispute?

I googled Shelby's name and clicked images. She smiled back at me in an array of happy times. I clicked on a photo from a charity event in October. Even in the still photo, Shelby was effervescent in her black strapless evening gown. Someone had called to her, and she'd looked over her shoulder, her blue eyes round and bright, an impish grin at the ready. Blonde, layered hair hung to her shoulders.

I clicked the arrow to the right to see the next image. Shelby in a polo shirt with a One80Place logo. Laughing children piled on top of her in an oversized beanbag chair.

Joy glowed from the goofy face she made. I wanted to think of her like this. This was the life that had been extinguished. I printed the photo and used a magnet to attach it to the top center of the case board Nate had set up in front of the fireplace.

Back at the computer, I put together a timeline of Shelby's life. "Interesting," I said. "Shelby went to Berkeley."

Nate looked up from the stacks he'd sorted onto one of the tables that now formed an "L" in the back left corner of the room. "I would've guessed somewhere more traditional. What did she study?"

"Sociology. With double minors in English and Philosophy. She came home in the spring of 1997 with a degree and Clint Gerhardt. They married the following May." I admired the photo I'd pulled from the newspaper archives. They sure looked happy. "They got married at St. Michael's Church."

"That the big white church at Meeting and Broad?"

"It is. One of the Four Corners of Law."

"Beg your pardon?"

"The intersection of Meeting and Broad has each of the Four Corners of Law. St. Michael's represents God's Law. The post office, federal law. The court house, state law. And city hall, local law. Robert Ripley—the *Believe it or Not* guy—named the intersection. Apparently it's a regulatory oddity."

"Well I'll be damned. Episcopal?"

"Yes, well, Anglican," I said.

"So they would've gone through all that premarital counseling we went through."

"Exactly."

"Seems like maybe the priest didn't see Clint as one of

Shelby's strays."

"Clearly not. And good grief, they'd been married for...eighteen years. Surely it wouldn't've lasted that long if he'd been merely a project for her."

"What's his background?" asked Nate.

"I'm working on it. Very different from hers." I read from three open windows on my screen—a city directory, a newspaper archive, and a subscription database. "He's five years older than she was. He grew up in Oakland, California. Joined the Army right out of high school. He was a Ranger when he and Shelby got married, and he didn't leave the Army until 2007."

"Where was he stationed?"

"Fort Benning, Georgia. I can't find any indication he's had a job since he was discharged."

"Interesting. When did they buy their house on Tradd Street?"

With a few clicks I was into the county real property records. "Before they were married. Right after Shelby came home from college. And it was titled to both of them, but I'd bet the money was hers." Property records were public information. Bank records weren't legally available.

"Parents have money?" asked Nate.

"Piles. They have three homes, one on East Battery. No mortgages. They're on several philanthropic boards. All the usual tells."

"They must've approved of Clint if they gave Shelby the money for a house on Tradd Street with her engaged to him. And Shelby and Clint would've had to've lived in Georgia ninety percent of the time for the first ten years they were married. I guess she came home when he was deployed.

Otherwise that house sat empty a lot."

I pondered that. "Maybe they were renovating it over time. And her parents may not have given her the money. She could have a trust from her grandparents. I need to dig some more. What did Paul Baker focus on? Can you tell yet?"

"So far all I've seen indicates he was convinced Shelby was having an affair."

"Oh no." How sad, if that were the case. I wanted to believe Clint and Shelby had still been as in love as they looked in their wedding photo. "With who?"

"I haven't run across anything yet to suggest he ever figured that part out. Looks like the solicitor's office maintains adultery was Clint's motive. Baker apparently spent a good deal of time trying to find this alleged lover. His working theory seems to've been that the paramour was maybe the culprit."

"And after four months of looking he couldn't find him?" I felt my face contort into one of those looks that causes Mamma to hold forth about wrinkles. "Maybe Shelby *wasn't* having an affair. What evidence is there that she was?"

"If any exists, and it's in these boxes, it's well hidden." Nate continued scanning and sorting folders. After a few moments he said, "Apparently our client gave Charleston PD the idea that Shelby was unfaithful."

"Hell's bells. What was he thinking? He surely didn't lawyer up right off. He could've caught her entertaining half the men South of Broad in her birthday suit and a lawyer wouldn't've let him breathe a word of it. Which makes me tend to believe he's innocent." I sighed. "We need to talk to him right after we talk to Fraser in the morning."

"Agreed. I'll make that call. He's at home with an ankle

monitor. At least we don't have to make a trip to the detention center."

"So he made bond. Any indication the family made a stink about him using marital assets to secure that?"

"None so far." Nate eyed a piece of paper on the top of a growing stack and tapped a number into his phone. After a few minutes, he ended the call. "He's not answering, and his voicemail box is full. He doesn't recognize my number. I wouldn't answer either if I were him. Probably thinks I'm a reporter. We'll get Fraser to make the introduction."

"Who all did Paul Baker talk to? Who did he suspect Shelby might be having an affair with?"

"Baker is apparently not as meticulous with his interview notes as we are. Also, his filing system is indecipherable." Nate picked up a file and flipped through the pages. After a while, he said, "Charles Kinloch. His wife, Jane, is a friend of Shelby's. He spent enough time alone with Shelby to raise suspicions."

"Whose suspicions? His wife's?"

"That's not on this page. Kinloch denied the affair, and he had an alibi for the night of the murder. He was in London on business, verified. I'm looking for what kind of business...What the...You won't believe this."

"What?"

"Baker went to London to check out that alibi."

"Sweet reason. You have got to be kidding me."

"Nope," Nate said. "Invoice is right here. He stayed at the same hotel Kinloch did—South Place Hotel. No wonder Baker's billed so much, if this is how he operates. We would've checked that alibi with a few phone calls."

"How long did Baker stay in London?"

"Three nights."

"That's just damn ridiculous. Looks like Fraser would've fired him right off."

"I think he did just that," said Nate. "This invoice appears to be the last one. Baker was in London last week."

"Okay, back to Charles Kinloch. If he was having an affair with Shelby that went sideways, he could've hired someone to kill her. But typically if it's a lover you're looking at a crime of passion. We need to see if he could've had any other motive. Who else?"

Nate flipped a page, skimming. "He seems to be the only candidate. But this file—Baker's investigation—is awfully thin. There's more legal motions in these boxes than anything else. Here's a rough outline of the Gerhardts' schedule the Sunday Shelby was killed." He walked over to the scanner, laid the document on the bed, and pressed a button.

A PDF appeared on my screen. I looked it over, then added it to the electronic case file. I started a profile on Charles Kinloch. He was a Charleston native with a pedigree. Graduated from Virginia Commonwealth University with a degree in Photography and Film. No criminal record, no civil complaints. "Kinloch is a self-employed photographer."

"The artsy kind, the newspaper kind, or the family portrait kind?"

"It's hard to tell. I think he does a little bit of everything." I kept digging.

Nate said, "Charleston PD, and later Paul Baker, interviewed the neighbors on both sides. Both reported hearing arguing once or twice, but nothing that caused them alarm. Both couples were home the night Shelby died, but neither saw anyone coming or going. Unfortunately, this strengthens the solicitor's assertion that Clint killed his wife. He was the only one there."

"What are their names, the neighbors? I want to talk to them."

"Nick and Margaret Venning, and Edward and Evelyn Izard."

I added them to my list and went back to creating profiles.

Nate and I worked until dinnertime, grabbed another sandwich, and sat on opposite ends of the sofa.

I said, "The timeline for the day Shelby died feels awfully lean."

"It was just another Sunday. They spent it the same way we spend a great many Sundays. They had breakfast, walked the dog—in their case, dogs, I guess, from what Fraser said—went to church, puttered around the house, had dinner, and then he went to his study and she went to the library."

"We would've both been in here," I said.

"True enough, but I don't think it necessarily means anything that they were in different rooms."

"Probably not," I said. "So he went to listen to music in his study. And she was reading."

"They were in for the night. Alarm was on stay," said Nate.

"Someone she wasn't expecting must've rang the doorbell. Clint didn't hear it because of the music. Shelby recognizes whoever it is, disarms the alarm system, and invites whoever it is up to the library, or maybe they follow her up there. There's an argument. The french doors are open because...okay, it was December. Why were the french doors open?"

"What was the weather on December 28?"

"I'll check," I said. "But they must've been open…there was an argument. The visitor pushed Shelby out the doors."

"That's one possible narrative. Another is maybe there wasn't an argument. Shelby's visitor had malice aforethought. In which case he or she must've come armed with a weapon of some ilk, or a plan to use something in the house. No one would've set out to kill her by pushing her out the french doors. Too iffy."

"True," I said. "Or it could've been an accident."

"You mean she fell? The coroner's report says she went out the doors backwards with force. Her back hit the rail. There was bruising. I guess she could've flung herself, but then we'd be looking at suicide, and that's not a very efficient way to get the job done."

"From the second floor, she could easily have survived that fall. If she hadn't hit her head so hard. Whoever is responsible, they would've had to've gone down to check to see if she was dead, right?"

"Hard to see it happening any other way," said Nate. "Either our culprit was checking to see if Shelby could be saved—in which case maybe they would've called 911. Or they were making sure she was dead."

"The only way this wasn't someone she knew well is if it was someone she'd just met and was trying to help."

"Maybe Shelby did take in the wrong stray after all."

"Maybe," I said. "But my money is on someone she knew."

"Shall we divide and conquer?"

"We'd best," I said. "We don't have much time. I want to talk to the folks at One80Place first thing in the morning."

"Maybe I'll go get an up-close view of Charles Kinloch. See what he's up to on a Wednesday morning. A self-employed photographer can mean a lot of things."

"True. We need to be at Fraser's at ten. Then I'll talk to Clint Gerhardt if you'll head over to One80Place."

"I thought you wanted to go there first thing," said Nate.

"I do. But I'm going to show my ID and ask questions. Would you like to volunteer to serve lunch? I can sign you up online."

Nate flashed me a conspiratorial grin. "Good idea. But tell me again why Colleen can't just find Shelby over in the next life and ask her what happened?"

I sighed.

Before I could open my mouth, Colleen popped in and solidified. When she solidified, she looked like any other person. She only did this when she had to for a case, maybe to serve as a distraction. Or when she wanted to eat.

"Fix me a chicken salad sandwich and I'll explain it to him again," she said.

I rolled my eyes. "Fine. But then we have to get back to work. We're nowhere close to finished going through these files, and I'll never get all these profiles finished tonight. We've got to know everything Fraser Rutledge knows about this case and more by first thing in the morning."

I headed to the kitchen while Colleen explained how the rules prohibited her from interfering with anything not part of her mission.

Nate had adjusted to her easier than I'd had any right to hope. I think he was mostly relieved that there was an explanation for some of my odd behavior.

# THREE

Nate and I took both cars to Charleston the next morning. I was at One8oPlace by seven forty-five. I parked my green hybrid Escape in front of the building and studied it. The tan, two-story brick facility with a red metal roof looked clean and modern. Bicycles were parked out front underneath the jaunty slanted portico. This didn't look like a homeless shelter to me. Perhaps that was the point.

The surrounding neighborhood was a mishmash of well-kept but modest homes, neglected homes, vacant lots enclosed by chain-link fences with barbed wire on top, and old industrial buildings of indeterminate use. An elevated section of I-26 floated a few hundred feet away.

Casting an eye around to make sure I was unobserved, I took my Sig 9 out of my Kate Spade tote and locked it inside a floor-mounted safe in the back of the Escape. I had an idea firearms weren't welcome inside the shelter.

When the lobby doors opened at eight, I went inside. I offered the woman at the front desk my sunniest smile, introduced myself, and showed her my PI license and ID.

The fifty-ish woman in the red One8oPlace logo shirt took me in from head to toe. In my denim skirt, blue gingham blouse, and white denim jacket, I probably didn't look like her idea of a private investigator. She smiled, but her eyes were wary. I got it. Homeless folks had enough problems. An investigator of any sort had the potential to bring trouble down on somebody.

"What can I help you with?" she said.

"I'm working on the Shelby Poinsett case. Shelby Gerhardt, I mean." If you were born a Poinsett in Charleston, you remained one even into the hereafter.

The woman's eyes saddened. "Such a tragedy. Shelby was a special person. We all loved her."

"I understand a lot of folks did. What exactly was her role here?" I asked.

"I think you should talk to Tricia Hopkins. She's our volunteer coordinator." She picked up the phone, turned her back to me, and spoke softly. When she hung up, she turned around and told me that Tricia would be right down.

I thanked her, wandered away from the desk, and took in the lobby. It was utilitarian, to be sure, with greyish beige walls and floors and nothing for purely decorative purposes. But the two-story glass entrance lent a sunny, optimistic air. A trio of what I assumed were staffers came through the door. A perky, petite brunette, a pale, chunky, red-headed guy, and a tall, muscled black man, all in One80Place logoed polo shirts, they were deep into a discussion. They smiled as they walked by.

"Good morning." A woman's voice came from behind me.

I turned to face the staircase. Tricia Hopkins was a well-dressed, late-thirties woman with light brown hair. As she got closer, intelligent eyes met mine. She could likely have been an executive at any number of Fortune 500 companies.

We shook hands, introduced ourselves.

"I understand you're here about Shelby?" she said.

"That's right. I was curious what her role here was."

"She was a volunteer. And a donor. We deeply miss her. I was under the impression an arrest had been made in her death."

"I'm working with her husband's defense attorney," I said.

She scrutinized me for a moment, seemed to think weighty thoughts. "Please, come upstairs to my office." She led the way.

I followed her up the staircase, through a set of glass doors, down a greyish beige hallway, and into her office.

"Have a seat." She moved behind her desk and I stepped in front of a visitors' chair. I couldn't help but contrast her office with Fraser Rutledge's. Her clients didn't have the deep pockets that his did.

Before I could sit all the way down, she said, "I don't mean to be blunt, Ms. Talbot, but I hope you aren't suggesting to the authorities that one of our guests was somehow involved in Shelby's death."

"Goodness, no," I said. "I just started working this case yesterday. I understand your organization was very important to Shelby. I'm trying to get to know her, as it were."

"But you wouldn't be here unless you suspected a connection to her death."

Tricia was sharp.

"Honestly, I'm still far too new to this case to suspect anything. But I have to start with where Shelby spent her time and that was, to a large degree, here. The sooner I can get a clear understanding of exactly what she did here and eliminate any plausible connection to her death, the sooner I can move on to other avenues of investigation."

She held my gaze. "Very well. Shelby would've made an excellent case manager. But we require a master's degree for that position. She was happy to do what she could, which was help out with some of our training programs, organize fundraisers, fill in at the front desk...She did a variety of things. She was willing to do whatever we needed her to do on any given day."

"To the best of your knowledge, did she ever involve herself in the affairs of the folks living in Tent City?"

A look of relief flashed across her face. This line of inquiry wasn't as close to home. "I honestly don't know. Shelby was such a giving person. She often pushed the boundaries here—wanted to be a part of things in a more hands-on way. Is it possible she ventured into Tent City in an effort to help, perhaps convince the campers to come to us? I'd have to say yes. That would certainly have been in character."

"I apologize," I said. "Do you have a ladies' room I could use?"

"Certainly," she said. "Just down the hall to the right."

"Excuse me. I'll be right back." I headed out of her office and down the hall, taking in the functional office space. I popped in and then immediately back out of the ladies' room. I scanned the corridor, not sure exactly what I was looking for. I just wanted a few unsupervised minutes to snoop. All the offices were occupied. No luck there. On the virtually unadorned wall, a bulletin board full of photos caught my eye. Was Shelby in any of them? I stepped over to take a look.

I scanned faces. There, in what looked like the cafeteria,

wearing an apron with a woman and two small children. And again, outside on the playground with a group of children. Happy, smiling. Shelby was making a face in one photo, to the apparent delight of three little girls.

And there she was again, in her One8oPlace logo t-shirt, with a very familiar face. Her arm was tucked behind his back, and his behind hers. Standing real close. They were eating ice cream cones and smiling for the camera.

Sonny Ravenel.

My brother Blake's lifelong best friend. Practically a member of our family.

Charleston Police detective.

I looked up and down the hall, removed the push pin, and tucked the photo in the pocket of my denim jacket.

What. The. Hell?

I scurried back to Tricia Hopkins' office, took a deep breath, and forced a neutral expression onto my face. "Thank you so much," I said.

"Not at all."

I returned to my seat. "Do you have a lot of community volunteers?"

"Yes, actually. We're very fortunate in that regard. Businesses help out with donations. It's not at all unusual for local restaurants to cook for the residents. And countless individuals give of their time every week."

"How about the local public service offices? Fire department? Police department?"

"Certainly. Individually and sometimes in groups." A confused look crossed her face.

"A friend of mine—he's a police detective—Sonny Ravenel. I think he's volunteered here before."

"It's certainly possible."

I stood. "Well. I've taken enough of your time. May I call you if I have further questions?"

"Of course." She handed me her card and walked me out.

In the car, I took a few deep breaths, then pulled out the photo and stared at it.

Ice cream. Kids romping all around. This couldn't be anything other than an innocent coincidence. I posed for photos with my arm around other folks' backs all the time. It didn't mean a thing.

Except the two of them looked so happy. And they were awfully close.

This was nothing. Nothing.

Damnation.

My iPhone sang out "Always Gonna Be You" by Kenny Chesney.

Nate.

"Hey," I answered.

"I've got unfortunate news," he said.

My insides clinched, braced for another blow. "What?"

"First, Charles Kinloch has a clear schedule, on this Wednesday morning anyway. Hasn't left the house. Came out in what looks like yesterday's clothes to get the paper earlier, but that's it. At any rate, while I've been watching him do nothing, I finished going through the last file from the last box."

"And?"

"Kinloch's business in London involved getting a money shot of a Kardashian. His alibi is airtight."

"We knew he had an alibi. What's the unfortunate news?"

Nate sighed. "Paul Baker was looking at Sonny Ravenel."

"Why?" My right hand, the one clutching the photo, trembled.

"According to Baker's notes, Delta Tisdale, another friend of Shelby's, suggested Sonny as a possibility because Shelby mentioned his name a lot. Apparently, she spent a good bit of time with him on behalf of folks at One80Place."

"Sonny would never be romantically involved with a married woman." I was talking to myself as much as Nate.

"Is he romantically involved with anyone?"

I pondered that for a moment. Here was a glimmer of hope. "Last I heard he was dating a girl from Folly Beach. He brought her to The Pirates' Den about a month ago, remember? It was a Friday night. The band was playing. I declare I don't remember her name." Sonny and my brother, Blake, along with a few of their friends, had a band—The Back Porch Prophets. They played most Friday nights at The Pirates' Den, a local favorite restaurant and bar. Blake played pedal steel guitar and keyboards. Sonny played guitar, sometimes drums depending on who all showed up to play. They all had day jobs.

"Brunette?" Nate asked.

"Yeah, short hair. She was real cute." As far as I knew, Sonny hadn't been serious about anyone in years. I couldn't stop staring at the photo.

"Liz—"

"Of course we need to talk to Sonny. And to this Delta Tisdale." Her name came out of my mouth like maybe she was someone who frequently reported zombie alien Sasquatches. "Anyone else on the suspected adulterer list?"

"No. Just Charles Kinloch and Sonny."

"If Paul Baker billed Fraser for four months, billed for a trip to London, and Sonny was the best idea he came up with, I don't blame Fraser for being pissed." I was feeling defensive of my friend and I knew it. I had to follow this wherever it led.

I finished the call with Nate and tapped Sonny's name in my favorites list. He answered on the third ring.

"How well did you know Shelby Poinsett?" I asked without preamble.

"Well I'm fine, Liz, how are you? How's married life treating you?" If the question rattled Sonny at all, it wasn't in his voice.

"This is serious."

"Why're you asking?"

"Nate and I are taking over the case for Paul Baker, investigating for Rutledge and Radcliffe."

"Is that right?" He went quiet, like he was giving the matter careful consideration.

"Answer the question, Sonny. How well did you know Shelby? Did you know Paul Baker was investigating you?"

"I would be a damn poor excuse for a detective if I couldn't pick up on that. He was asking questions around One8oPlace. I have friends there. Seems like Baker had some fantasy maybe I knew Shelby a little too well."

"Did you?" I maybe sounded a little crazy. I was staring at his smiling face in that picture.

"Seriously, Liz?"

"Sonny, I have to ask. This was his primary line of investigation—that Shelby was having an affair. His theory was that her lover killed her. Your name is one of two in his file, and the other guy has an ironclad alibi."

"Yeah, and when Paul Baker mentioned that crap theory to Bissell and Jenkins, we all had a good laugh about it. Rutledge and Radcliffe ought to get a refund." Sonny sighed, muttered something. "Shelby and I were good friends. Have been for years. She volunteered at One80Place. So did I. But as someone who is also my good friend, you know damn good and well I don't date married women. Besides that, Shelby was crazy about her husband. I told Paul Baker as much. I guess he didn't believe me because he thought that served my interests. But it's the truth."

I sat back, relaxed. Only then I realized how I'd been coiled tight as a spring. "I had to ask."

"Yeah, I get that."

"So if Shelby wasn't having an affair—"

"No one ever thought she was except Clint. And now Bissell and Jenkins, the solicitor, and Paul Baker. To hear Shelby tell it, Clint's a good guy, but insecure. Held on a little too tight to Shelby. Hell, he probably knew she was way out of his league from day one. Shelby, she talked about him all the time, and her face lit up when she said his name. I'd bet my favorite Gibson guitar she was not having an affair."

"But who else besides a lover would come inside her house at nine o'clock at night, throw her out the french doors, and leave without her husband ever knowing they were there?"

"If I knew the answer to that, you wouldn't have a new case."

"How well do you know Clint?" I asked.

"Never met him. Everything I know about him came from Shelby. Bissell and Jenkins are convinced he killed her. I hate to think that, the way she loved him. But there just isn't another reasonable theory of the crime."

"I'll let you know when we find one."

I ended the call without asking him about the picture. I pulled a notebook from my tote and tucked the photo inside the pages. It was nothing. There were children there, for Heaven's sake.

I would keep right on telling myself that for as long as I could.

# FOUR

Our meeting with Fraser was brief. Nate and I were exhausted, but up to speed. We had no questions for Fraser at that juncture and weren't ready to share any observations. Fraser was thankfully due in court. He called Clint Gerhardt and asked if I could come by. From Fraser's end of the conversation, Clint was unenthusiastic. But he agreed and asked that I get it over with.

I kissed Nate goodbye, and he set out for One80Place. Because the Gerhardt home was only a five-minute walk from Rutledge and Radcliffe, I left my car parked on Broad and headed towards the Old Exchange and Provost Dungeon. Across East Bay, the massive yellow stone building seemed to stand guard over the foot of Broad Street. It was hard to walk past it without recalling that the Declaration of Independence had been presented to citizens from the steps. Walking through Charleston was like stepping back in time, if you ignored all the cars.

I turned right on East Bay, enjoying the bright blue sky and the Cooper River peeking at me between buildings on my left. As soon as I crossed Elliott, a horse-drawn carriage full of tourists pulled to a stop at the curb, the guide explaining the history of Rainbow Row. This cheerful line of historic houses painted Caribbean pink, yellow, blue, and green with their wrought iron balconies and window boxes spilling over with flowers always made me smile.

I crossed Tradd, then turned right and walked up its left-hand sidewalk, against traffic. Most of Tradd Street, including this end, was a one-way street by car. It was a narrow lane crowded with street parking on my right. Several times I had to thread myself between window boxes and crepe myrtle trees planted in sidewalk cutouts. On both sides of the street, I caught glimpses over courtyards and through garden gates.

I slowed my pace as I approached the Gerhardt home. You could always get a better perspective on things by foot, especially walking in a direction you couldn't drive. It was a three-story brick townhouse, flush with the stucco house to the right—the Izard home. A short brick driveway on the left ended just past the side entrance where the house, which at first appeared rectangular, bumped out into an L-shape. A wrought iron gate allowed access to a pathway, but the gnarled branches of a live oak obscured anything beyond. The courtyard must've been behind the house.

The neighbors' house to the left sat back from the street, with a courtyard out front. The Venning driveway ran adjacent to the Gerhardt driveway, leaving space between the houses. Many of the homes on Tradd Street dated to the late 1700s. Like quite a few of the others, the Gerhardt home was so close to the street the front door was virtually on the sidewalk.

I rang the bell and waited in front of the recessed, glossy black door with a fanlight above. A runner approached from my right. Dressed in high-end running shoes and togs, electric blue Oakley sunglasses with what looked like wings on the frames, a fitness watch, and an arm band for his smartphone, he could've been taping a commercial for one of several advertisers in *Running World* or some such publication.

He stopped next door, nodded at me, and slipped a key into the lock. Mr. Izard, I presumed.

The door in front of me opened and I got my first glimpse of Clint Gerhardt. Tall and solid, he had close-cropped reddish brown hair, agitated blue eyes, and enough facial scruff that I couldn't be sure if he'd forgotten to shave for a few days or if this was his look. His jeans and button-down shirt were pressed. "Liz Talbot?" he asked.

"It's a pleasure to meet you, Mr. Gerhardt."

"The name's Clint." He stepped back to let me in. Multiple dogs barked from somewhere upstairs. "Let's talk in the kitchen. You want coffee?"

"Sure, thanks." This wouldn't be an easy conversation. Something to fiddle with would be good for both of us.

I followed him down the side hall towards the back of the house. From what I could see, the home had been tastefully decorated and beautifully maintained. Soft ivory walls, gleaming heart of pine floors, and traditional furnishings greeted me. I caught a glimpse of a large portrait of Shelby over the fireplace as we passed the living room.

The kitchen had been recently modernized, with white custom cabinets, marble counters, and all new appliances. It was spotless. Not what I'd expected, given he was living alone under house arrest.

"Have a seat." Clint nodded towards a table in front of a set of french doors that led to the brick-walled courtyard.

Oh dear Heaven. We were going to chat while looking at

the very spot Shelby had died.

"You take cream and sugar?" he asked.

"Yes, please." It was a lovely courtyard. Plants burst from the built-in beds and ivy covered one of the walls. A swimming pool sat against the far side with a fountain spilling into it from the wall.

The kitchen table was round with four chairs. I took the one facing the courtyard. Clint brought me a mug of coffee, then sat across the table from me.

"Thank you," I said. "You have a lovely home."

"Shelby," he said by way of explanation.

I nodded and sipped my coffee. Strong and rich with plenty of cream and sugar. "This is delicious."

He waited silently for me to get to the task at hand. For a moment I kept quiet too. Sometimes silence made guilty people uncomfortable, gave them the impulse to fill it with chatter. Was Clint guilty, or was he another victim of someone else's crime?

After a few minutes of a strange version of quiet chicken, I said, "I know this must be difficult for you. I apologize for asking you to talk about it again."

"Difficult." He looked at me squarely, his grief a palpable thing, an aura emitted through his eyes from the core of his soul. His tone was soft, matter of fact. "Shelby was my whole world. I don't even know how to get through the day."

"I'm terribly sorry for your loss. I give you my word I will do everything in my power to find out who killed Shelby and why."

"That won't bring her back."

"No," I said. "It won't. But it will keep you out of prison, or worse."

"Trust me, worse is here. It doesn't get worse from Shelby being dead."

I held his gaze. In that quiet moment, I knew in my bones he hadn't killed his wife. It was more than the pain he wore. Killers often missed their victims. But Clint Gerhardt impressed me as that rare creature completely without artifice, an upright man, a squared-away soldier.

My resolve to find out the truth of what had happened here hardened.

"Mr. Gerhardt—Clint, I've read the file. I've learned a thing or two about your wife. And I have a husband who I adore myself. I can tell you this for absolute certain: Shelby would not want you to go to prison. She wouldn't want you to stand trial. She would want you to live a full and happy life. And as remote as that possibility must seem to you right now, the best way to honor her is to try to do what you know she would want."

He looked away for a moment, then nodded.

"Is it all right with you if I record our conversation? I can focus and take fewer notes."

"Sure."

I tapped the Voice Memo app, then the record button, and laid my phone on the table. I pulled out my notebook and a pen just in case I thought of something I wanted to remember to follow up on later.

"I have it on good authority that your wife was crazy about you. Can you tell me what in the name of sweet reason made you think she was having an affair?"

He winced, looked at the ceiling, then shook his head. "Part of me could never believe she picked me. Eighteen years of marriage. She was a perfect wife. So much more than

I ever deserved. But I grew up poor. Our worlds couldn't be more different. Sometimes she'd be out working at One8oPlace—she spent a lot of time there—or at the Library Society, wherever. I'd start thinking about men she grew up with who maybe volunteered there too. She never gave me a reason. But this feeling I'd never be good enough for her, it ate at me. Once in a while I'd get a wild hair. Think maybe she was seeing someone. Then she'd talk me down and we'd be all right. It was a cycle."

"And you were in one of these—cycles?"

He nodded.

"And you decided it was prudent to share this with Charleston PD?"

"I was in shock. I wasn't thinking it could make me look guilty. I was thinking I wanted them to find who killed Shelby."

"Anything out of the ordinary that triggered your recent suspicions?"

"Not really. She was spending a lot of time at the shelter. Working with homeless women and children." He drew a slow breath, stared at his coffee mug. "We weren't able to have children. Shelby...the doctors said we could've tried fertility treatments, procedures. They had a long list of things they were eager to do to her. But Shelby said no. If God didn't choose to give us children, He had a perfectly good reason, and maybe she was supposed to love other children who needed extra.

"We talked about adopting, but to be blunt, I wasn't as convinced as Shelby that I was parent material. My role models were far from ideal. Shelby found other outlets for her maternal instincts. Lately, there was one little girl she talked about a lot. Her and her mother. The father was abusive."

"Do you recall the little girl's name?" If Shelby had wound up in the middle of a domestic violence case, that could easily have gotten her killed.

"Kelly. Her mother's name is Sonya."

"Did you ever volunteer at One80Place?"

He drew a long breath, then blew it out and shook his head. "I'm an idiot. I didn't want her to think I didn't trust her. Didn't want to be too clingy, smother her. She wanted me to be happy, to do whatever I was interested in. It would've made her happy, if I'd've gone."

"So what do you do?"

"I build houses." A fat orange tabby sashayed up and rubbed against Clint's legs. Absently, Clint reached down to scratch behind the cat's ears.

"What a pretty kitty. My grandmother had one who looked just like him. His name was Roscoe."

"This is Socrates."

"He clearly loves you."

"Ah, he just wants a treat." He continued to pet the cat, who rolled over and assumed the universal "I want a tummy rub" position.

"Where were we?...You went into construction when you got out of the Army?"

"You could say that, I guess. I doubt anyone would pay me, but I'm dependable. I work with Habitat for Humanity. In my spare time I've been working on fixing up a sailboat I have docked over at Charleston Harbor."

"Tell me about the day Shelby died."

He recounted exactly what Nate and I had been over the

night before from his last Sunday with Shelby.

"Was it typical for you to spend evenings in separate rooms?" I asked.

He shrugged. "Occasionally. Shelby had book club business she needed to work on."

"Book club?"

"Yeah, aside from One8oPlace and family, that took most of her time. Shelby was a reader. Loved books. The ladies around here...I don't know how book clubs normally work. But these women take their book club seriously. Shelby was president. They have a treasurer, a secretary, the whole bit."

This didn't sound anything like my book club, which was more of a social group where we drank wine, ate hors d'oeuvres, and chatted about a great many things, including the book of the month. "Sounds formal."

"It is. Most of Shelby's close friends are in it. It's like...more than a hundred years old. You have to be invited to join." His face announced his disdain.

"So she had book club business and was in the library on the second floor?"

"That's right. Just above where we're sitting."

"And you were listening to music on the third floor?"

"Yeah. I have a vinyl collection in my study."

"Did you have on headphones?"

"No. But I closed the door. The acoustics are better with the door closed." He swallowed, took on a sick look. "It's an acoustic door. It's designed to keep noise out."

"Did anyone have a key to your house aside from you and Shelby? A maid, any other staff?"

"No one. I'm very security conscious. We've got the best

deadbolts made. Only Shelby and I had keys. There's a spare set hidden in each of our cars, and one in the safe deposit box."

"With respect, even the best deadbolt locks can easily be picked by anyone who Googles how. There're YouTube videos demonstrating how it's done."

"That's why the locks are backed up by floor-mounted door barricades when we're home. And of course we have a security system, which was armed in 'stay' mode when I went upstairs. No one could've opened either door except Shelby."

"Who set the alarm? You, or Shelby?" I asked.

"I did."

"Would it be in Shelby's character to let someone in the house she didn't know well? Someone new at the shelter?"

He shook his head. "Absolutely not. Shelby had a heart of gold, but she wasn't stupid. She wouldn't have opened the door for someone she didn't know. We had an incident a few years back. Someone showed up begging at the door. Shelby was here by herself. She called me and I came home and got the guy a cab to the shelter."

"But what if it was someone she knew from the shelter?"

"A client?"

"Yes." Or her client's husband.

"She wouldn't let them in. We talked though all of that. We had protocols."

"So by process of elimination, Shelby was killed by a friend or family member." I looked at him directly.

"So it would seem." His words came out bitter.

"Any thoughts on that?"

"None. Everyone we knew loved Shelby. It's impossible for me to imagine any of them would hurt her under any circumstances."

"Something unimaginable happened here," I said. "I need the names of everyone you can think of who Shelby would've let in the front door."

"All right...well, her parents. Williams and Tallulah."

"Did she get along well with them? Do you?"

"Yeah. They're great people, warm, down-to-earth. Like Shelby. She was close to them. So am I. We had dinner there most Sundays."

"That Sunday?"

"No. Tallulah had a cold. She missed church. Seems like they had a church dinner planned that night anyway."

"You all attended church together?"

"Well, we're all members of the same church—St. Michael's. And we typically sit together, so I guess, yeah."

"What about Shelby's brother, Thomas?"

"She wasn't close to him. He's all about power, position, money. He lives in San Francisco. Hasn't been home in years. Until the funeral."

"Are the family financial arrangements such that he would benefit from Shelby's death?"

"No. They both have trusts. Shelby and I jointly owned hers. I'm the only one who benefits financially."

"Who established the trusts originally?"

"Shelby's parents. Hers was modified after we were married."

"What about their estate?"

He took a long swig of coffee, then set his mug down, raised an eyebrow. "They're both in good health. But when they pass, a chunk of the estate goes to various charities. The remainder is owned by a trust. Shelby and Thomas were beneficiaries. But Shelby's share…I don't see that going to Thomas. They'll probably divert that to charities important to Shelby—One80Place. The church. Charleston Library Society. Animal Rescue."

"Any other family?"

"Shelby's grandparents are at Bishop Gadsden retirement home—her mom's parents. Her dad's parents passed five years ago."

"That's it?"

"She has a few cousins in Atlanta. Aunts, uncles. But they don't stay in touch."

"None of them ever asked her for money?" Family that didn't stay in touch might reach out if they needed something.

"They all have plenty of their own."

"There are no deep dark family secrets? I'm not going to find out that Shelby had a dramatic childhood incident with an uncle—nothing like that?"

"Oh God, no."

"So in your opinion, no one in Shelby's family had a motive to kill her?"

"I'd bet my life on it."

I looked at him for a long time. I didn't have to tell him that was exactly what he was doing. "What about your family?" I'd already profiled Clint and his family. But I wanted to hear what he had to say.

"What about them?" He took a long drink of coffee.

"Are they still in California?"

"My parents are. I have a brother, Cliff. He's stationed at Fort Benning."

"Are the two of you close?"

"Yeah. He has a wife and two daughters. They were all crazy about Shelby."

"Did you see them at Christmas?"

"They were here for a week. Santa came here to see the kids."

"You didn't see your parents during the holidays, neither you nor your brother?" I asked.

"No." His face went hard. "Shelby made damn sure my parents were taken care of. Against my wishes. But they aren't much on family." Clint's parents, Bill and Brenda Gerhardt, had both been to prison on drug-related charges. He and his brother had been in and out of foster care growing up. I knew this. It was in the file.

"Any chance they would show up here looking to be taken care of better?"

He was quiet for a long moment. "I wouldn't rule it out."

"What about friends?"

"Shelby's best friend is—was—Jane Kinloch."

"Kinloch? She married to Charles Kinloch?"

"That's right." He looked away.

"Any idea where Paul Baker got the idea Shelby was having an affair with Charles?"

"That would've been me." A pained look crept across his face. "They had coffee together a lot. And he had a way of watching her I didn't care for. We had dinner with them about once a week."

"He was in London when Shelby died. If he had anything to do with it, he would've had to've had an accomplice or hired it out. That doesn't feel right to me. Do you disagree? Is there any reason I should give him a closer look?"

"No more or less than anyone else we knew," he said.

"You socialize with Fraser Rutledge and his wife as well?"

"Yeah. Shelby and Fraser were tight since the schoolyard. His wife, Constance, I'm not sure she was happy about that, how close they were."

"She the jealous type?"

Clint made a face. "I don't know. Maybe. Fraser's all talk. He acts like he's always chasing something, but my take is he's a family man. They have five kids. She would destroy him in a divorce. No one knows that better than Fraser."

"Who were Shelby's other friends?"

"Delta Tisdale. She's the secretary of the book club. Mariel Camp, Anne Spence, Erin Guidici, Liz Bell, and Mary Bernard. They're in the book club too. So's the lady next door—Evelyn Izard. She and Shelby weren't close, though. Evelyn is a notorious lush. The other women in that club I don't know. Jane or Delta could tell you."

"What about your neighbors on the other side?"

"The Vennings? Nick and Margaret. We don't—we didn't—spend much time with them."

"Some of the neighbors told the police detectives they'd heard you and Shelby arguing."

"Fraser mentioned that. Honestly, I don't know what they were talking about. Maybe they heard the TV. Shelby and I didn't yell at each other—ever. And the Izards...it's as likely as anything the Vennings heard the Izards fighting and thought it was us. But who knows? The most likely way any of us could overhear any of the others would be outside in the courtyards."

I mulled that for a minute. "Does your courtyard back up to the lot behind you?"

"Yeah. There's an old carriage house on the other side of our courtyard wall. I don't think anyone's living there."

I made myself a note to follow up to be sure. "Any other friends you can think of?" Had he known Shelby was close to Sonny?

He shook his head slowly. "That's it. The staff at One80Place—that's all online. Shelby talked about most of them at one time or another."

"How about folks she knew at church?"

"There's overlap there. Jane and several of the book club ladies go to our church. Shelby had so many friends. But the one she spent most of her time with, that would be Jane."

"Was Shelby a member of a gym?" I asked.

He shook his head. "No."

"Was she a part of any other group that you can think of? Did she stay in touch with friends from college?"

Skepticism twisted Clint's face into a scowl. "Not really. She exchanged Christmas and birthday cards with a few of them. Emails, an occasional phone call. But for one of them to show up here, that would really be out of the blue."

"But possible?"

"Highly improbable, but possible, I suppose."

"I need every name you can recall."

"Her roommate was Lark Littleton. The other names are in her address book. I'll get it for you before you leave."

"What about friends from Georgia? Your Army buddies?"

"We were close with the guys in my unit and their wives. But I've been out for nearly eight years. We see them all once or twice a year." He shook his head, drew back his lips in something that approached a sneer. "No. Just, no."

"Are they still active duty?"

"Two of them are."

"May I please have their names, phone numbers, and current cities just so I can eliminate them?" Military records—recent ones—were virtually impossible for me to access legally. I had no inclination to access them illegally.

"It's pointless, but fine." He called out five names, looked up the phone numbers in his phone. I took everything down.

"Can you think of anyone else Shelby would've opened the door to without coming to get you?"

He was silent for a long time, stared at nothing over my right shoulder. "No. That's it. But you'll never convince me one of our friends or someone in our family killed her."

"I really hope you're wrong about that. Let's switch channels for a moment. Why would she've had the french doors open in December, do you suppose?"

"It had been a warm day—in the low seventies. Shelby's hot natured. She was always opening those doors to let in fresh air," he said.

"Are the library doors not tied into the alarm system?"

"Yeah," he said. "She punched in her code and bypassed them."

"Is it possible she just turned the alarm off before she opened the doors?" I asked.

"No. Every time one of us types in a code, it's recorded at the alarm company. She bypassed the library doors right after I went upstairs. She disarmed the system at 8:55 to let someone in."

"I know this is obvious, but I have to make sure I'm asking the right questions, which means I need to ask them all. Was Shelby having trouble with anyone?"

He looked at his coffee, shook his head. "No. Nothing serious."

"What do you mean?"

"I'm about to step into it, I know. Women...you get a group of them together, and there's always squabbles."

I raised an eyebrow at him.

"You know exactly what I mean." He sounded exasperated.

I did know what he meant. "Okay, so who was squabbling?"

"The book club ladies. Minor stuff. You'll have to ask Jane."

"Do you have her cell number?"

He pulled out his phone, looked it up, and rattled it off.

"What about you?" I asked.

"What do you mean?"

"Were you having trouble with anyone? Is there anyone from your past who might have a grudge? I know this is far-fetched, but is there anyone who might bear you animosity from your time in the military?"

"Plenty of people. But they're on other continents and don't know my name or how to find me."

"How about from California? People you knew years ago?"

"No," he said. "No one. But it doesn't matter. Because these are folks Shelby never laid eyes on. She wouldn't have disarmed the alarm system, released the floor barricade, and opened the door. She would've come straight upstairs to get me."

"Okay. I think I have what I need, except I'd like to take a look around if you don't mind."

"Sure. I'll give you the tour. You came in through the front." He stood and headed through the butler's pantry and into the dining room. It was furnished with what I'd bet were expensive antiques, but like the living room beyond, nothing about it was ostentatious. The rooms were uncluttered, with only framed family photos on the occasional chest or table.

I followed him to the third floor. On the front of the house overlooking the street, his study was all dark woods and leather, with a sofa floated near the center of the room, its back to the door. A desk in front of the window faced the sofa, and shelving for countless vinyl record albums lined the walls. Beside the desk was a stout-looking metal stand which held a turntable the likes of which I'd never seen. It appeared both futuristic and antique, retro shiny metal with a glossy wood-grained top and an actual spinning platform that looked at least four inches thick. I must've been staring at it.

"It's a Continuum Audio Labs Caliburn," he said. "Shelby bought it for me for Christmas years ago. It was unlike her, the extravagance. That system probably cost a hundred grand. She'd never spend that on herself for something purely for entertainment."

"It's beautiful," I said.

He almost smiled. "It is that."

His study, like the rest of the house, was immaculate. "Is someone coming to clean for you? Cook?" We moved down the hall.

"Nah. I don't mind cleaning. Gives me something to do. The women from the church keep my freezer stocked. Two or three of them are by here every week to check on me. Tallulah too. I don't have much of an appetite."

One of the guest rooms was open. I peeked in as he

passed towards the closed door at the back of the house. The dogs barked louder.

"Do you want to meet the dogs?" he asked.

"Sure."

He tilted his head, raised an eyebrow, and opened the door. Five dogs, one small, three medium, and one very large, all of mixed breeds, rushed Clint. The small one, who likely had some Yorkshire terrier in her, ran around Clint in a circle. Two others jumped up and put their front paws on his legs. The large dog, which might have been part English Mastiff, part St. Bernard, sat with his tongue hanging out and watched the others.

Clint ruffled heads, patted sides. "Hey buddies. Good boy. Good girl. This is Scooter, Gertie, Gladys, Blue, and Bear."

The Jack Russell Terrier mix sprang from the floor straight up in the air repeatedly, like a bouncing ball.

"Scooter, you rascal. You'll get to go outside soon." For the first time that day, Clint smiled.

Bear woofed once. He wanted attention too.

They were all so happy to see Clint, they barely noticed me.

Finally, a shepherd mix cocked his head at me as if to say, "Who are you?" Then they all came to say hello.

"Okay now, don't jump on her."

"They're fine." I laughed, patted heads, and scratched them behind their ears. Bear lumbered over and pushed his way through the crowd. "Sweet puppies."

After a few moments, Clint gentled them back into the bedroom and closed the door.

"Someone come to walk the dogs?" I doubted his ankle

monitor allowed him to do that.

"I hired a service."

We went back to the second floor. I followed him into the master suite. Done in shades of white, ivory, and taupe, it was luxurious and restful. Scattered across Shelby's skirted dressing table were things she likely held precious: framed photos, perfume bottles, a silver ring holder with a pair of diamond earrings, a pressed flower. On the tufted chair was a sleeping striped cat that might've been a Maine Coon.

"That's Plato," said Clint.

The Gerhardts each had a walk-in closet.

"Have you gone through her things?" I asked. "For any clue as to someone who might have meant her harm?"

"That's all I've done. There's nothing here."

I pondered that. If other leads didn't materialize, I would come back and repeat the search.

We stopped at the door to the library. "You don't have to come in here," I said.

"I don't mind. I feel close to Shelby in here. This was her space. Her books, her things." He sat in a buttery leather chair by the fireplace and put his feet up on a matching ottoman. "This was her reading spot."

Built-in bookcases lined the walls from floor to ceiling, wrapping over the doors. A large writing desk sat several feet inside the french doors, facing the room. The space had the feel of a traditional library, but with feminine touches. Fresh-cut yellow tulips in a crystal vase brightened the corner of the desk.

"Yellow tulips were her favorite," he said. "They've delivered them once a week ever since we settled here permanently after I got out of the army. I can't bring myself to stop the delivery."

I swallowed hard and nodded. "Where were the dogs?"

"With me. They like jazz. They were sprawled all over the rug."

"Was anything in here disturbed?"

"Only one thing I could find."

I turned towards him.

"Her desk calendar. The page for that Sunday was torn out."

"That seems important. She didn't mention she was expecting anyone?"

"No. But just that one page was gone."

"Did the police follow up on that?"

"Honestly, I think they would've if they'd thought of a way. They seem like decent guys. But things looked cut and dried from their perspective. Can't say I blame them. In the end, they said I probably destroyed it in an attempt to throw suspicion somewhere else. I did not."

"Did she keep an electronic calendar?"

"No. Shelby led an unplugged life. She had an iPhone for safety because I insisted. She would've carried the simplest model of phone you can still buy. She didn't use her phone for email. She didn't use social media at all. But I wanted her to have access to directions when she needed them. And the Find My Friends app so I could locate her. Shelby habited parts of town that could be dangerous. I wanted to keep her safe."

"And keep tabs on her?"

He scowled. "No."

"But you did, didn't you? When you were in one of your cycles? It would've been very tempting."

"Okay, so maybe I did." His voice was soft, sounded like regret. "But that's not why I wanted her to have the phone."

"Did you ever find her somewhere other than where she said she was going to be?"

He stared at his hands. "Yes, I did."

"More than once?"

He nodded.

"Where was she?"

"Several different restaurants around town. And Market Pavilion Hotel."

I absorbed that for a moment. "They have a restaurant there. And two bars."

"They do."

"Where did she say she was?"

"She'd be somewhere else, and then on the way home she'd make a stop she forgot to mention."

"Did you ever ask her about it?"

"No."

"Why not?" I asked.

"Because in all the years I knew her, I never knew Shelby to lie. I was afraid I might not want to hear the truth." His voice was tight with pain.

I gave him a moment. Shelby's calendar was still open on her desk. The police hadn't even taken it. I flipped through the pages. "Can I take this?"

He cleared his throat. "Sure. Her address book is in the top desk drawer. I think you needed that."

I reached for the drawer handles, confirming permission with an asking glance.

He nodded.

I slid open the drawer and pulled the leather-bound

address book that matched the calendar out. "I'll get this back to you."

"No rush."

I stepped over to the french doors. The bookcases framed them, recessing them from the room. There was no balcony, only a window ledge and a wrought iron rail that came up to my waist. I tried hard to imagine how someone might accidentally fall out the doors and over the sturdy barrier. My imagination failed me.

"How tall was Shelby?" I asked.

"Five-seven. Not quite as tall as you, but almost."

"Could we walk outside?" I asked.

"Of course." He seemed to steel himself.

We went down the stairs, back through the kitchen, and into the courtyard. The pool was the focal point. A variety of green plants thrived in deep planters in each corner. Water splashing from the fountain into the pool made a soothing sound. Such a peaceful oasis. Such a horrible thing happened here.

The front end of the walled garden was grass. A wooden doghouse sat under a canvas sun shade.

"Only one doghouse?" I asked, thinking that could lead to fights.

"That's Annabelle's. All the pets sleep inside. But Annabelle needs more time outdoors during the day than the others."

"Annabelle? You have another dog?"

"Belly isn't a dog." On cue, a large, black-and-white potbellied pig appeared from behind the house. "She's dug a spot in the yard behind the house where she likes to sit during the day."

I'm an animal lover from way back. But I took a moment to process two cats, five dogs, and a pot-bellied pig in a townhouse. Fraser was right. It was a petting zoo.

Belly meandered in our direction.

"She can be territorial where I'm concerned." Clint took a step away from me. "She won't bite you."

Belly laid down in front of Clint and rolled over for a tummy rub, just like Socrates had done earlier in the kitchen. Clint knelt to oblige the pig. "Belly's a sweet girl."

"It's good you have company." I kept both eyes on Belly, who very likely outweighed me. "I'm just going to look around. Is there access from outside?"

"Yes." He pointed to the kitchen corner of the house. "There's a pathway around back that leads to the driveway. You can't see it until you're right in front of it."

I took in the six-foot brick wall. If someone had come down to either verify that Shelby was dead or try to help her, they'd come through the kitchen or down the path. I walked over and peered behind the house. The space was only wide enough for the walkway. I meandered back towards Clint, scanned the courtyard again

"I've troubled you enough for one day," I said. "May I call you if I have questions?"

"Of course." He gave Belly a final pat and stood. He called out his number, and I typed it into my phone and added a contact. Then I gave him my number and Nate's so he'd know who was calling and answer the phone.

He escorted me back to the front door and opened it.

I said, "For what it's worth, you've got yourself one more believer."

He met my gaze. "I appreciate that."

I couldn't get it out of my head how odd it was he hadn't mentioned Sonny. One of Shelby's friends—Delta Tisdale— gave his name to Paul Baker because Shelby talked about Sonny a lot. I was out the front door. In a moment Clint would close it behind me. I had to ask while I could see his face.

"One more thing," I said. "Do you recall Shelby ever mentioning Sonny Ravenel?"

He pressed his lips together, shook his head. "The name is vaguely familiar. But he's not one of Shelby's friends far as I know. Why?" If he wasn't being candid, he was a superb liar.

"He's a friend of mine who volunteers at One8oPlace. I thought maybe they knew each other." Sonny's name would be familiar to many folks in Charleston from crime coverage in the news.

"She never mentioned him. Most people who volunteer serve meals in the community kitchen. I bet that's what your friend does. Shelby was a long-term volunteer. She spent most of her time at the women and children's shelter."

I smiled. "That explains it."

Except it didn't. Why wouldn't Shelby mention Sonny to her husband if he was her friend? Who all else had she failed to mention? What kind of secrets did Shelby have?

# FIVE

Shelby's best friend, Jane Kinloch, agreed to meet with me, but suggested lunch at The Park Café instead of me dropping by her Hampton Park Terrace home. I had mixed emotions about this arrangement. I would learn more about Jane and her husband, Charles, with a visit to their house, where family photos, mementos, and other artifacts of their lives would be on display.

But The Park Café was a pretty lunch spot. It was situated at the approximate intersection of three upper peninsula Charleston neighborhoods: Hampton Park Terrace, Wagener Terrace, and North Central. Big windows, lots of natural light, a crisp, white-on-white décor, and a plethora of plants made it comfortable and inviting. And the menu offered what Nate, Sonny, or Blake would've called girl food.

While I waited on the banquette side of a table in the corner, I opened the Voice Memo app on my iPhone, tapped the red button to record, then pressed the home button to return to the menu. I laid my phone on the table, the way I often did in restaurants to keep it handy. Jane would likely never notice the thin red bar at the top that said "Recording." Typically I asked before recording a conversation. But in some cases, my instincts told me the subject might be skittish of such a thing. I would be asking Jane to talk candidly about her husband and her friends.

A trim blonde dressed in white slacks and a yellow blouse with a colorful scarf walked through the door, searching the room with her eyes. I waved. She nodded and headed my way. Her hair flipped up at the shoulder, a few bangs scattered across her forehead. She touched her pearls as she approached the table.

"Jane?" I asked.

"Yes. You must be Liz. So nice to meet you." Her voice identified her as a card-carrying sweet Southern lady.

"Nice to meet you," I said. "Thank you so much for coming on such short notice."

"I hope you'll forgive me for not having you to my home." She slid into the chair across from me.

I was thinking how she'd wanted the option to end the conversation whenever she pleased without the stress of having to invent a sufficient excuse to get me out of her house or risk being impolite by asking me to leave.

Her voice dropped to a near whisper. Her hazel eyes shimmered. "It's just that...I've done this several times now. The police, Clint's attorney, his investigator—the first one. And now you. I would do anything I could to help Shelby. To help Clint. But I really don't know anything helpful. And this brings it all back."

"I am so sorry for asking you to do this. But I need to get up to speed fast. They'll start picking a jury in two weeks."

Jane pressed both sets of fingers to her lips, closed her eyes, and nodded.

"You said you wanted to help Clint. So you don't believe he killed Shelby?" I asked.

"Oh good Heavens, no. Such a thing is simply not possible. I worry about him, you know? He positively cherished her."

"But not to the point of obsession?"

"Was it healthy for him, how much his life revolved around hers? I wouldn't presume to pass judgement on that. But I know this much. He'd sooner rip his heart out with his bare hands than hurt her. And you should know *this*. Shelby was like a sister to me. If I thought there was a remote possibility he'd done this, I'd pull the switch to fry him myself."

The waitress stopped by to see if we were ready to order.

"I know what I want," I said. "Do you?"

"Yes." Jane turned to the waitress. "I'd like The Park Lettuces with chicken and an avocado toast. Unsweetened tea, please."

I smiled. "I'll have the same, but I'd also like the field pea hummus. Want to share?"

Jane smiled back. "I just love that stuff."

The waitress collected our menus and slipped away.

I pulled the Purell out of my purse, pumped a generous pool into my left hand, set the sanitizer on the table, and rubbed my hands together, making sure to get my forearms. I looked up to see Jane watching me. "Would you like some?"

"No thank you," she said. "I just washed my hands."

I resisted the urge to tell her how many people had handled the menus, and changed the subject. "I had to give up sweet tea when I turned thirty." There may have been longing in my voice.

Jane gave a little moan of despair. "Me too. The calories. Just wait 'til you turn forty."

"You can't possibly be forty." Of course I knew exactly how old she was.

"I'm every day of it, and feeling it lately." She gave me a long, searching look. "I have to tell you, if you're thinking my husband was having an affair with Shelby, you're barking up the wrong tree. That other detective, he just wouldn't let go of that notion. It's no wonder he never got anywhere."

"We've already eliminated that so-called lead." This was mostly true.

"Really?" She tilted her head. "Well, maybe you will find out what happened to Shelby. I tried to tell him Charles and Shelby were just friends. The three of us have known each other all our lives."

"I've heard they had coffee a lot, Charles and Shelby. Anything in particular they needed to discuss? Were they working on some committee together?"

"No," she said. "Nothing like that. We had a few rough spots, Charles and me. He...Charles grew up with money. But we've had to work for everything we have. Neither his parents nor mine handed us a trust. We have a good life. But it eats at Charles that some of our friends have homes South of Broad and we don't. Shelby was a good friend to both of us. She spent extra time with him, tried to make him see how unimportant material things were."

"So you never thought there was anything going on between them?" Aside from ruling Charles completely out, I needed to vet Jane.

"She was my best friend since childhood. It's just not possible she would ever betray me like that."

I nodded, held her gaze. I didn't know her well enough to know how good a liar she was, but I was inclined to believe her. "This is purely a formality, you understand. For my files. Goodness gracious—all this paperwork. I have to check everyone off. Where were you the night Shelby was killed, at around nine o'clock?"

Jane flushed. Her hand fluttered up to her chest. "Now...now...you can't possibly think—"

"Oh, of course not. Why, everyone knows you were her very best friend. I just have to document it. For the files."

"Well, I was at home. With the children. We have a twelve-year-old boy and a ten-year-old girl."

"And Charles was in London. What a shame he had to travel over the weekend, right there between Christmas and New Years. Is that typical?"

"Charles works all the time. We were lucky he was home Christmas Eve and Christmas Day."

"What does he do?" Of course I knew the answer. But I wanted to hear how she would characterize his job.

"He's a photojournalist. He does freelance work for newspapers, magazines...all like that."

"I bet he does have crazy hours." His photo credits suggested paparazzi might be a more accurate term than photojournalist. The shot he'd taken of one of the Kardashians the night of Shelby's murder was date and time stamped. It was his alibi—unless he'd had an accomplice. I wanted to believe the Kinlochs were innocent. But until we uncovered the truth, everything was a possibility.

"What about Sonny Ravenel?" I asked.

Jane stilled. "What about him?"

"How well did Shelby know him?"

"They were friends. Shelby met him at One80Place."

The waitress placed our iced teas in front of us.

"Did she talk about him a lot?"

Jane lifted a shoulder. "She mentioned him sometimes."

"Were Shelby and Clint happily married?"

"Very. They were devoted to each other."

"Do you think it's possible Shelby was having an affair, not with Charles, but with anyone? And before you answer, remember that Clint's very life depends on us getting to the truth. We're way past protecting reputations here."

Jane sipped her tea. She set the glass down and smoothed the edges of the napkin under it. "It's possible." The words were almost a whisper.

"Tell me what you know and what you suspect." I kept my voice gentle.

"You have to understand who Shelby was. She had such a big heart. But she never lived by anyone's rules but her own. She was a free spirit, a bit of a wild child when we were younger."

I kept quiet, let her talk.

"She was crazy about Clint, would never have left him. But Clint kept Shelby on a pedestal. He treated her like a china doll. There was a side of her that craved excitement. If someone pursued her...maybe someone a little dangerous...she might've had a fling."

"Did you ever know her to do this?" A meaningless affair seemed inconsistent with the nearly angelic image of Shelby I had so far.

Jane shook her head. "She wouldn't have told me. It's not the kind of thing she would've told anyone. Shelby would've seen that as disloyal to Clint, the telling."

Interesting. I sipped my tea. Either Shelby had been a complex woman, or Jane had an agenda of her own.

"I'm not saying she had an affair," said Jane. "I'm saying it's possible. And if she did, it wasn't anything serious."

"But the other person involved might not have felt the same way," I said.

"Exactly. That's the only reason I'm telling you. It feels like a disgraceful breach of her trust. But I know she'd want me to help Clint if I can."

"If she were having an affair, could you venture a guess as to who it might've been with?"

Jane mulled that for a moment. "The only person I've heard her talk about who isn't a part of our circle is Sonny. That's the thing. It would never have been someone from inside our circle. That would've been a violation of family almost."

Something grabbed my insides and twisted. Sonny just couldn't be a part of this. I tried mightily to wrap my brain around Shelby's code.

Jane said, "I'm afraid I've explained things badly. I wouldn't want you to think poorly of Shelby. She was a beautiful spirit."

I nodded, sipped my tea. "Do you think Clint knew Shelby had this wild streak?"

Jane was quiet for a moment. "He probably saw it. Maybe sometimes she'd want to kick up her heels—dance in the rain in her evening gown, or skinny dip late at night in a hotel pool—harmless things. Sometimes he went along with her. Sometimes she pushed him past his comfort zone, I think. But yeah, he knew her very well."

"How do you think he would've responded if she did have an affair and he found out about it?" I asked.

"I think it would've killed him. But he still would never

have hurt her. I don't care what she did."

"What if he confronted her, they fought, and it was an accident?" I asked.

"Honestly? I don't think he would've confronted her. I think he would've known it was just her on a tear. Talking about it would've made it real. As long as he never mentioned it, he could pretend it never happened. But that's assuming she had an affair to begin with. I'm not convinced she did."

The waitress set our lunch in front of us. We oohed over it—men just don't appreciate pretty food the way women do—then commenced tasting.

After a few bites, I asked, "How did Shelby get along with her parents? Her brother?"

"She was very close to her parents. They're such sweet folks. Like second parents to me. Thomas has been an insufferable ass his entire life. As much as Thomas has, he always wants more. More money. More power. Friends in high places—he's a shameless name-dropper. I suppose Shelby loved him. He was her brother, after all. But they just lived separate lives."

"Can you think of any family rift that might've escalated? Sometimes money makes folks act out of character."

"Not at all. In fact, if you didn't know the Poinsetts had money, you'd never guess it from the way they act. Well, except for Thomas and his wife, Deirdre. And Shelby never mentioned them at all. There wasn't anything to fight over, really. Williams and Tallulah were smart. Or maybe they had good advisors. Everything to do with the money was decided years ago. If there was a way for Thomas to get more of it, I wouldn't put it past him to try. I'm not saying he'd kill Shelby, now. But he's a manipulator. My sense is that

Williams and Tallulah understood money can corrupt people. They took steps early on to make sure it never came between their family."

"How did they respond to Clint when Shelby first brought him home?" I asked.

Jane smiled. "Oh, I expect Williams had him checked out thoroughly. Probably hired a team of investigators the first time Shelby mentioned his name, long before she brought him home. By the time he showed up in Charleston with Shelby, the Poinsetts knew everything there was to know about Clint Gerhardt. But Williams has a lot of respect for Clint. That's Williams. He admires anyone who overcomes adversity. And Tallulah...she could tell—anyone could—that Clint adored Shelby. That's all that mattered to her."

"So there was never any drama there?"

"Never. I think the Poinsetts sort of adopted Clint. They became the parents he never had. You know what I mean."

"What about Clint's real parents? Did Shelby ever mention them? Did they contact her, ask for money?"

"Those two." Jane rolled her eyes. "They didn't need to ask Shelby for money. Her accountant sent it to them regularly. She bought them a house, a new car every few years. She never dealt with them directly, mind you. The accountant handled it all. The stipulation was that they leave Clint alone—never ask him for anything, never contact him unless he initiated it. And they had to stay away from drugs, anything illegal."

"Did those arrangements continue after her death?"

"Yes. She set them up their own trust. It's modest, as those things go. But still, they'll never have to worry about money."

"What about Clint's brother, Cliff?"

"Oh, he's a sweetheart. He and his wife Lisa and their two girls...Shelby was crazy about them. Cliff is Clint's twin, you know."

"I don't think anyone mentioned it."

"Identical."

I tucked that away to ponder later. "Was Shelby giving them money too? Does Clint?"

"Oh my goodness, no. Clint's parents are leeches. But Cliff would never take a dime from Shelby. He's just like Clint."

I tilted my head and squinted at her, thinking how that didn't square with the reality that Clint had clearly benefitted financially from marrying Shelby.

Jane lowered her chin and regarded me from under raised eyebrows. "You're thinking Clint cared about Shelby's money?"

"I wouldn't know if he cared about it or not. But he's the recipient of most of it."

"When they first met? Shelby was at Berkeley. One reason she went so far away to school was to experience life outside wealth and privilege. She saw it as a burden. No one there knew she came from money. She didn't want to be treated differently because of it. Of course this was more than twenty years ago—back before everything about everyone was on the internet."

"So you're saying Clint didn't know she had money when they were dating?"

"He had no idea until after he'd proposed. Knowing Clint, he wouldn't've gone out with her to begin with if he'd known. When she told him, at first he was so angry he broke off the engagement. I guess he felt like she'd deceived him. Honesty is very important to Clint. I suppose it's important to any relationship. But Shelby had her reasons for what she did. And in the end he loved her too much to walk away. She convinced him that money didn't have to change their relationship. They didn't let it."

"And Cliff—"

"Loved Shelby for Shelby, not her money. Just like Clint."

I nodded, then forked a bite of salad and delivered it to my mouth.

Jane said, "But just to be clear, if Cliff and Lisa ever needed anything—if one of the girls got sick, Heaven forbid—whatever. Shelby would've helped. She would've insisted on it. Don't waste your time looking at Cliff and Lisa."

"All right," I said. "Did Shelby stay in touch with her friends from Berkeley? Her roommate? Other friends?"

"Not really. Not in recent years anyway. When Clint and Shelby were spending most of their time in Georgia, I guess it's possible. But I really don't think so. Shelby fully invested in building a life with Clint. She was close to Lisa, Cliff's wife. And the wives of the men in Clint's unit at one time, though I think they've drifted apart since Clint got out of the army."

"How did that work—after Shelby and Clint got married, with him in the army? I know they bought the house before they got married."

"That's right. They spent years tinkering with it, living here when Clint was on leave. Shelby was ready to be back in Charleston. Having the house and working on it made her happy, even though they couldn't spend much time here for so long."

"Was Shelby at odds with anyone that you know of?"

Jane laughed. "Oh my goodness, was she ever."

I scrunched my face at her. This would've been good information right off.

"Oh," she said. "No, no...nothing like that. Nothing that someone would kill her over. It's just, your question made me think of book club."

"Book club?"

Jane laid down her fork. "The Ashley Cooper Book Club. It's more than a hundred years old. There are eighteen of us—that's the limit. It's in our bylaws. There are twenty on the waiting list. In order to be added to the waiting list, you have to be nominated by a member and voted on."

"Sounds exclusive. So what was the trouble?"

"Shelby was president. She'd just been installed in September, and it was quite controversial."

"What was the controversy?"

"Like I said, Shelby was unconventional. This club is very traditional. Some of the members' great-grandmothers were founders. They take book club very seriously—it's part of their heritage."

"How did Shelby get elected president?"

"Everyone loved her. Even the women who called her hippy-dippy behind her back did it with a little smile."

"So how did the trouble start?"

"Well, Angela McConnell is on the waiting list—she's a sweetheart, only twenty-eight. She's engaged to Mary Bernard's son, Lamar. Mary Bernard's great-grandmother was the original president. Mary wanted to let Angela move from the wait list to active. Her logic was that not everyone came to every meeting, so why not let Angela participate."

"That seems reasonable."

"But not to Mariel Camp, whose friend has been on the waiting list longer. Nor to many of the members who don't like change. At least half the ladies wanted to keep with tradition."

"And which side was Shelby on?"

"She was going to call it to a vote."

"That seems fair."

"It does, doesn't it? But you would be amazed at how many members were affronted by this. I declare, you'd've thought children's lives were at stake, the way some of these women carried on."

"You're not serious?"

"Oh, but I am. Some folks need more to occupy their time."

"I'm going to need all their names and contact information."

Her face contorted into a scandalized look. "No, seriously. These ladies aren't murderers. A couple of them are grandmothers, for goodness sake."

"That's not a disqualifier."

"Really, please don't waste your time on this. I didn't tell you about it because I thought any of these ladies were *suspects*. Your question just reminded me of all the brouhaha."

I gentled my tone. "My goodness, I'm not saying they're suspects. But they may well know something helpful."

Jane took a bite of her salad and chewed thoughtfully.

"Who is the president now?" I asked.

"Delta Tisdale."

The zombie alien Sasquatch reporter. "When is the next

meeting?"

Jane paled. "Tomorrow at noon. It's a luncheon."

"Where?"

"Well, it's at Delta's house, but—"

It would save me an enormous amount of time if I could meet them all at once. "Are you allowed to take guests?"

"Well, yes, but I'm telling you, none of these women could possibly have killed Shelby."

"Unfortunately, I'm going to have to investigate several impossible things. Because one of them is the truth."

# SIX

Right after Nate and I came back from our honeymoon, we made our own protocol of not discussing cases over meals or in the bedroom except in the most urgent circumstances. Most of our clients were in tough situations. Our natural instincts were to work continuously until we solved the problem at hand. But that could lead to burnout. It would be too easy for work to take over our lives. We made a pact to take care of us. The day before, we'd had no choice but to break the rules.

That Wednesday night we cooked together. The kitchen was one of my favorite rooms in the sprawling beach house I'd inherited from Gram. It was a chef's kitchen—Gram had loved to cook, the bigger the crowd the better. Painted green cabinets, two farmhouse sinks, and a wood floor lent the space a homey feel. Copper pots hung above the black granite island and lined the open shelves beneath the commercial-grade gas stove. I'd spent a chunk of my childhood under Gram's feet in this kitchen.

Nate threw together a salad and boiled angel hair pasta while I sautéed bite-sized pieces of chicken in butter and olive oil. Rhett trotted over to where I stood in front of the stove, sat, and looked up at me hopefully.

"All right. One bite of chicken." I placed a chunk I'd

cooled especially for him on a paper towel and set it on the floor.

He scarfed it down, sweeping his tail back and forth on the floor. Then he resumed the hopeful look.

"How about some kibble?" I asked.

Nate laid down the salad tongs and walked over to pet Rhett. "Come on, boy," Nate said.

Rhett followed him into the mudroom.

I heard the scoop in the dog food canister. Nate carried on a one-sided conversation with Rhett while he fed and watered him. I smiled at his matter-of-fact tone, as if Rhett understood him completely. It was the same way I spoke to Rhett.

After a few minutes, Nate came back into the kitchen. Because he's well acquainted with my fondness for good hygiene—which certain members of my family unkindly refer to as my germaphobia—he washed his hands thoroughly. He cast me a sideways grin as he slathered on the Purell. "Sanitized for your protection."

I smothered a smile, removed the browned chicken from the pan, added garlic, and stirred.

"Mmm. That's smelling fine," said Nate.

"Well, thank you."

"And to think your mamma worries you don't feed me right."

"There are a great many things I don't do to Mamma's standards."

He moved behind me, lifted my hair, and kissed my neck. "And yet you so spectacularly exceed all of mine."

I smiled, keeping my eyes on the pan with great effort.

"I suppose I'd best let you be...for now."

The promise in his voice sent shivers of desire through every fiber of me.

He moved away.

"Tease," I said.

"You know better."

I did indeed. I took a deep, slow breath, so as not to ruin dinner. I scooped the chicken onto a plate, then added chicken broth, white wine, and lemon juice to the pan, stirred to deglaze, and watched the liquid reduce.

I turned off the heat, added spinach and halved grape tomatoes to the pan, then added back the chicken. Once everything was combined, I poured it over the pasta bowl, added parmesan cheese, and tossed it all together.

Nate opened a bottle of Murphy-Goode pinot noir, poured us each a glass, and set them by our places at the farmhouse table. I took the pasta bowl and joined him there. Over dinner we flirted with each other, exchanged tidbits of island news, stared out the window at the ocean, and took time to appreciate the meal we'd prepared.

Only after we'd cleared the table and taken our wine to the living room did we turn back to our case. In some ways I felt guilty, as I always did, setting the client aside for a while. But coming back to a case with a fresh perspective often yielded clarity.

I grabbed Shelby's address book and my notebook from my tote. We settled into opposite ends of the sofa, facing each other with our legs stretched out. I told Nate about my visit to One80Place. Like I was handling C-4 explosives, I passed him the photo.

He stared at it, winced. "This could be nothing more than a picture of two dedicated volunteers enjoying time with the kids. Someone says, 'Y'all smile for the camera.' They move in close and pose. Nothing to it."

"Or..."

Nate shook his head, a worried look in his eyes. "My opinion, they're cuddled up tighter than was strictly necessary for a quick snapshot. It's possible something was going on between them. We have to follow this down whatever rabbit hole it goes."

"I know." The pressure in my chest grew, rose into my throat. I spoke sternly to myself. I had to remain objective. There was simply no other option.

I filled Nate in on my interviews with Clint and Jane. Talking through the high points of what they'd said helped me feel like I had a better sense of things.

"I'm as convinced as Fraser that Clint is innocent," I said.

"All right. Why? Because he loves animals, volunteers with Habitat for Humanity, and hasn't canceled his wife's tulip delivery?"

"It's not just that. He strikes me as an honorable man."

Nate grimaced. "That, Slugger, is an emotional response to what could've been a carefully orchestrated performance."

"I can't see that being the case. He got very little notice I was coming."

"Let's set Clint aside for now, why don't we? What about the best friend whose husband mighta been having an affair with Shelby?"

"I'd place Jane and Charles Kinloch on the highly unlikely but possible list for now."

"I didn't find anything remotely resembling a lead today," Nate said. "Everyone I talked to claimed everybody loved Shelby. They're all in shock. But I don't think we can rule out someone Shelby knew through One8oPlace—or potentially Tent City—or any of the other organizations she volunteered at for that matter."

"Based on what Clint described as the 'protocols' at their house, I don't see our culprit being a client. Shelby wouldn't've opened the door for one of them."

"Unless it was a desperate one she'd worked with for a while and felt like she knew. This was an empathetic woman, from everything we've learned. She might've followed protocols right up until she didn't."

"That's true enough, I guess."

"We're running against the clock," he said. "There's a long list of people to sift through in two weeks. I think me working the volunteer angle makes sense. But that leaves you with a slew of friends and family."

Colleen popped in. She sat sideways in one of the wingbacks, her legs draped over the arm. Tonight's sundress was yellow, no hat.

Nate startled a bit. "For crying out loud. Could you ring a bell or something to alert us before you just appear like that? Normal people ring the doorbell. How about that? These constant shocks to our systems can't be good for our hearts."

Colleen waved a hand dismissively. "You'll get used to it. Eventually. You've got a strong heart. It's a shame I can't go along and help rule out a few of these people. I'm kinda busy right now."

I scrunched up my face at her. "With what? Is there something going on here on the island that I don't know about?" I hadn't caught wind of any new development plans.

"Nothing I need your help with," she said. "But if I get a free minute, I'll pop in while you're interviewing these folks. I can't promise. But I'll try."

Nate looked confused. "I thought you couldn't help because there's no connection to your day job."

"Weeeell..." she said. "Sometimes if I genuinely have nothing else I should be doing, I might bend the rules and pop in just for a minute. But you can't depend on that."

"Yeah, I'm abundantly clear on that part," said Nate.

"I could really use you," I said. "On the surface, at least, Shelby was a good person. She had nice friends, a nice family. But it would've had to've been a friend or family member—someone she trusted at any rate, knew well enough to open the door for—who killed her. That points to some extraordinary event, I think. Something went horribly wrong for these folks on an otherwise normal day. No one is going to volunteer this information to me, no matter how sweet I ask. Someone will be lying. Everyone else will be telling the truth. I need you, Colleen, to be my lie detector."

She blurred, went a bit transparent. "Your instincts are good. Follow them."

I said, "Okay, see? This drives me nuts. Does this mean you'll be there putting thoughts in my head and I won't even know it? Are you giving me a cryptic message? Or is that a simple compliment delivered with dramatic effect?"

Colleen returned to a semi-solid form, shrugged. She looked all innocent. "I just mean you have good instincts."

I blew out a breath. "Oh good grief. Where were we?"

Nate took a long drink of wine. "Lamenting Shelby's universal popularity, hence this long list of possible suspects."

It was my turn to drink. "And her circle of friends crisscrossed through church, neighbors, her book club, and her volunteer work. According to Jane, the only person from outside their circle Shelby has mentioned is Sonny."

"Are you going to talk to him again or do you want me to have a go at it?"

"I'll do it. But I want to dig a little deeper first. I have no reason to think Sonny wasn't telling me the truth. I'm going to the Ashley Cooper Book Club meeting with Jane tomorrow morning," I said.

"You don't seriously suspect these ladies in the book club, do you?" he asked.

"Of killing her?" I weighed that. "Probably not. But these women were Shelby's closest friends. A book club whose members have ties that go back generations? These women know all each other's secrets. I need to infiltrate the group. See what I can find out."

Nate raised an eyebrow. "I guess that makes sense. It's an efficient way to gather information."

"The problem is there are no good suspects. We have to eliminate them all one by one."

"I see your point, but some are more likely than others. Maybe we should prioritize."

"We can rule out random violence," I said. "Since we know what happened, and we have a finite list of suspects, it's a matter of figuring out which of those suspects had motive, means, and opportunity."

"No, this definitely wasn't random," said Colleen.

Nate and I both stared at her.

"What?" she said. "I'm picking up this stuff from you guys. If the Guardian Spirit thing doesn't work out, I can be a detective." Her laugh, a bray-snort racket that I maintained sounded like a donkey cross-bred with a pig, filled the room.

I rolled my eyes and tossed Nate Shelby's address book. Then I moved to the whiteboard and picked up a marker. "We need a list of possibilities. The way I see it, the most likely scenario is Shelby was having an affair, and her lover killed her either in a crime of passion or to keep the affair secret." Below and to the left of Shelby's photo, I started our list with "Unknown lover" in the suspect column and beside it made motive columns, "Crime of Passion" and "To Keep a Secret."

"At present, the candidates for lover are Charles Kinloch and Sonny," said Nate.

I cringed, but wrote the two names under "Unknown Lover."

"Jealousy would be a related motive," I said. "It could've been a wannabe lover, or maybe a different kind of jealousy."

"You mean like one of her friends was jealous that she...what...was beautiful, wealthy, popular, president of the book club?" Nate's face contorted with high skepticism.

I said, "I doubt that scenario would've been a premeditated murder, but it's possible jealousy led to an argument that ended up with Shelby in the courtyard."

"I guess if road rage is a thing, book club rage makes just as much sense," said Nate.

"So much more sense," said Colleen. "You have no idea how mean girls can be to each other. Women, I mean."

I swallowed a hot bundle of regret I carried for not standing up better for Colleen in high school. She'd gone through an awkward stage. If I'd been a better friend, she might not have gotten desperate enough to take her own life. "Colleen's right."

"You ladies understand the species much better than I

ever will," said Nate. "But could a woman have pushed Shelby with sufficient force to send her over a waist-high railing at the velocity the coroner stipulates?"

"If she was mad enough?" I said. "I think so. Another possible motive for the book club women would be to maintain the status quo—anger, for shorthand. Shelby was open to changes many of them didn't want." I added it to our board.

Nate said, "Also in the jealousy column, it could've been the spouse of someone who pined for Shelby."

"Good point," I said. "That would be the Jane Kinloch column."

"Or what if Sonny had a jealous girlfriend?" said Colleen.

I lifted a shoulder. I was still feeling tender towards Colleen. "It's a long shot, but possible."

Nate said, "My opinion, after hearing what Clint told you, the most likely scenario is Shelby got in the middle of a domestic violence situation and the husband of one of the women in the shelter came looking for Shelby."

I wrote "Angry Shelter Husband" in the suspect column and "Revenge" and "Prevent intervention" in the motive columns. "I think we have to check into it, but Clint was adamant Shelby wouldn't've let anyone connected to the shelter in the house."

"You mentioned that," said Nate. "But you and I both know people do things you don't expect them to all the time."

"Agreed. We have to run it down. Did you sign up to volunteer again tomorrow at the shelter?"

"Yes, and Friday. I'm also having a late lunch with some of the other volunteers tomorrow."

"Would you see what the folks at One8oPlace know

about this Sonya and her daughter Kelly?"

"Sure thing," Nate said. "So, working from the people closest to her out, the people we know Shelby would've let in the door, but who have no known motive to kill her, are her parents, her brother or his wife..."

We batted names back and forth. Nate flipped through Shelby's address book and I listed her remaining friends and family on the board.

"I see the roommate—Lark Littleton," said Nate. "If this is current, she's in San Francisco. But there are a few females I can't place. They could be college friends, local, or from anywhere Shelby's been her whole life."

I sighed. "I need to go through that with her mother. I'd hoped we could leave Shelby's parents in peace. I'll put them on my priority list."

When we thought we had everyone on the case board, I stepped back to review.

| Suspect | Motives |
| --- | --- |
| Unknown Lover | Crime of passion/Keep a secret |
|     Charles Kinloch | |
|     Sonny Ravenel | |
| Unknown Wannabe Lover | Jealousy |
| Spouse of Lover/Wannabe | Jealousy |
|     Jane Kinloch | |
|     Girlfriend of Sonny's | |
|     Girlfriend of Unsub | |
| Book Club Member | Jealousy/Anger |
|     Delta Tisdale | |
|     Mary Bernard | |
|     Mariel Camp | |

Anne Spence
Erin Guidici
Liz Bell
Evelyn Izard
Nine other members
Angry Shelter Husband     Revenge/Prevent interference
Williams or Tallulah Poinsett
Thomas or Deirdre Poinsett
Cliff or Lisa Gerhardt
Bill or Brenda Gerhardt
Fraser or Constance Rutledge
Members of St. Michael's Church
Clint's army buddies
Evelyn or Edward Izard (Neighbors)
Nick or Margaret Venning (Neighbors)
Board, staff, volunteers, clients at One80Place
Resident of Tent City
Board, staff, members of Charleston Library Society
Board, staff of Charleston Animal Society
Lark Littleton
Other college friends
Anyone unaccounted for in address book

"Damnation," I said. "That's crazy. I say we work the most unlikely ones first and eliminate them. Looking at that long list is making me itch. We need to erase some names fast."

"Try not to look at it too much. I think we have to start with the most likely scenarios," said Nate.

"You're right," I said. "It just looks so overwhelming."

"Most of these people we'll never even have to talk to,"

said Nate. "How about this? You work from the inside out—the people closest to her—and I'll start at the outer edges, with the long shots and the folks associated with the shelter."

"That sounds like a plan."

"Who's Unsub?" asked Colleen.

"What, you don't watch *Law & Order* and whatnot?" asked Nate.

"It means 'unknown subject,'" I said. "It's shorthand. The board's getting crowded. I didn't list out Clint's army buddies and their wives either, but I have their names and contact info."

Nate said, "I'd say those are outliers. I'll take them. But...someone is notably missing."

I glanced at Colleen. "My instincts tell me Clint is innocent."

Nate grimaced. "I'm as big a fan of your instincts as Colleen here. But I'd prefer to have something a bit more concrete before we rule him out completely."

"Fair enough." I added Clint's name with "Jealousy," "Money," and "Freedom" as possible motives. "From a purely clinical standpoint, if Clint killed her, and I don't for a single moment believe he did, his motive could've been to be free of Shelby but keep her money. If he divorced her—no. Nate, her trust, the one her parents set up for her? He told me it was redone when they were married. He jointly owns it. In that case, if they divorced, he'd get half. Right?"

"That likely depends on the way the trust was set up," Nate said. "That's a question for whoever modified it. Or her parents could tell you. But what if he wanted it all?"

I shook my head. "I think we're wasting time on Clint."

"We need to keep him on the list until we can cross him

off." His expression changed. He stared into space for a moment. "Upon further reflection, our job—what we were hired to do—is to find alternate theories of the crime."

I flinched. "I'm well aware of who's paying our bill and what he wants. But I will always see Shelby as the client. I want justice for her no matter what. But if looking at it that way makes you okay with crossing Clint off our list, then let's go with that."

"As you wish," said Nate. "But I don't like it. That's the one bad thing about working with attorneys. You're not necessarily hired to find the truth."

I erased Clint and all his possible motives.

"What if it was an accident?" asked Colleen.

"That's just not possible," I said. "Her injuries are inconsistent with an accidental fall."

Colleen persisted. "But what if someone was arguing with her and in the heat of the argument, they backed her up against the rail and she tripped?"

I pointed to "Anger." "Then whoever that was can tell it to the judge, but they're still responsible to some degree for Shelby's death."

"Gotta go," said Colleen. She faded out.

"What does she need to do at..." I looked at my watch. "Nine fifteen at night?"

Nate's expression said, *You can't seriously be asking me that.* "We need to talk about money. Shelby had a lot of it."

"That is one of the more common motives for dispatching someone to the hereafter," I said. "But Clint was very clear that he was the only one who benefitted financially from her death."

Nate rolled his lips inward, tilted his head, raised an

eyebrow. He wanted Clint's name on that board, no doubt. "Well, all right, then."

"All right then. Our plan of attack is this: I'm chasing down the uncorroborated affair with improbable or unknown subjects, and you're looking for Sonya's husband, sussing out if anyone at the shelter had a motive, and clearing some of the improbable names off our board."

"Looks like," said Nate.

We both stared at the board for a few moments gathering our thoughts.

"Here's the thing," I said. "Paul Baker. Something's not right there."

"What do you mean?" said Nate.

"We know him by reputation, right?"

"Right."

"But he's always had a good reputation. Why all of a sudden is he taking ridiculous trips to London and spending four months spinning his wheels?"

Nate was quiet for a moment. "You're thinking someone paid him to find nothing. He took Fraser's money and someone else's as well."

"All I'm doing right now is wondering."

"Fair enough. Maybe we should investigate the investigator."

"This feels like a lead," I said. "Everything on this board, it's the result of starting from nothing and puzzling out possibilities. But this feels like a thread we can pull. Maybe Paul Baker can be persuaded or tricked into pointing us in the right direction. I think I'll talk to him after the book club meeting tomorrow."

"And *I* think we've done enough for tonight. We were up

'til the wee hours last night going through those files. What say we turn in early?" His eyes told me exactly what was on his mind, and it wasn't sleep. He stood, set his wineglass on the coffee table, and walked towards me with intentions.

"I need to type up my interview notes while they're fresh. So do you."

He was standing in front of me. He touched my face, his eyes claiming mine. For a long moment, we stood drinking each other in. "That'll keep 'til tomorrow." He leaned down and kissed me so sweet, I lost all inclination to press my case.


Rain hammered the roof. Wind tore at the windows. I sat up in bed. What time was it? The room was dark. No glowing numbers on the alarm clock.

"We have to go." Nate, fully dressed and wearing his raincoat, strode towards the bedroom door.

"What do you mean?"

"The storm changed path. All the forecasts were wrong. It's gaining strength. Nearly a hundred and sixty mile-an-hour winds now. Category Five. This island will be underwater in a few hours. Storm's gonna make landfall at high tide. I'll get the kids. Get dressed and meet me downstairs. Hurry."

"Kids?"

"Hurry, Liz."

I threw on jeans and a t-shirt, grabbed a jacket.

I dashed to the bottom of the stairs.

Nate waited with two children I'd never seen before. A boy maybe five, a girl about three.

"Nate..."

"Let's go."

He opened the door, picked up both children, and dashed for the car.

I followed him into the jowls of a great howling monster of a storm, the likes of which I'd never seen. Trees were down, others bending near to breaking in the wind. I could barely walk against it. Rain pummeled us.

"Get in." Nate yelled over the wind. He put one child down to pry a back door open.

I tugged at the passenger door. When I got it open a crack, the wind caught it and flung it all the way open so hard I thought for a second it had blown off.

Nate was in the driver's seat, his door closed. "Can you get it?"

"I think so." I climbed out and pulled it with me as I climbed back in.

As soon as the door was shut, Nate hit the gas. The car flew out the driveway. Nate dodged downed trees and branches.

"Rhett!" I screamed. "Where's Rhett?"

Nate cast me an astonished look. "You're not good and awake yet."

I turned to the children in the backseat who couldn't possibly be mine, no matter how groggy I was. I wasn't able to have children.

Their bright eyes were round with fright, but they were silent.

"You must be right," I said.

Nate turned right on Ocean Boulevard and drove hell-bent around the north point of the island.

"Where are we going?" I asked.

"The ferry went down in the channel. It was overloaded. Everyone's trying to get off the island. We're going to have to take our boat."

"We have a boat?"

Nate kept his eyes on the road. We plowed through debris in the road, and more of it flying at the car.

A lawn chair hit the windshield.

Instinctively, I held up my arms.

Nate drove on.

We pulled into the marina parking lot. It was so crowded with cars I couldn't even see the docks.

Hundreds of people were fighting against the wind to reach boats.

"Where did all these people come from?" I asked.

"Can you take Emma Rae?"

The girl was named for my grandmother—for Gram.

I nodded, tears in my eyes. I had no idea who this child was.

I somehow managed to get out of the car, open the door, and gather her in my arms. Nate appeared at my side with the little boy without a name. "Link your arm through mine."

I did as he said, then clutched Emma Rae to me. We moved forward, locked together against the storm.

After what felt like hours, we made it to what I supposed was our boat slip. We boarded a thirty-foot cabin cruiser. The wind and the waves pounded and tore at us. The boat bobbed, slammed against the dock.

Nate said, "Take the kids below. I'll get us underway." He sat the boy on the deck and the boy wrapped his arms around my legs.

Then people I've never seen before started pouring onto

the boat.

On all sides, every boat I could see was being rushed by throngs of people.

"The boat will sink," Nate hollered. "It can't hold all of us."

A wall of water surged over the deck and we started to sink.

Then Nate was gone.

Had he washed overboard?

The children screamed.

"Nate!" I howled. "Nate!"

"Slugger. What is it?"

I was sitting in our bed, Nate beside me. I gulped in great lungfuls of air, clutched at him.

"You must've had a doozy of a dream," Nate said gently. "Are you awake now?"

"I know. I know."

"What, sweetheart?"

"I know why she's here."

"Who?"

"Colleen. I know why she's here. It's nothing to do with the environment. It never has been. There's no bridge. How will we all get off the island in a storm if there are too many of us?"

# SEVEN

Thursday morning came early. I hadn't slept well at all after the nightmare woke me. I was quiet during our run. Nate waited patiently for me to be ready to talk about it. Normally this time of year I'd grab a quick swim. But I was shaken in a way I've seldom been. I looked at the ocean with suspicion, reluctant to get in. I'd always loved the water. As a child I fantasized about being a mermaid.

I wanted to dismiss the dream as simply a garden-variety nightmare. But the truth was, all my life I'd had dreams that foreshadowed the future. Not all of them, of course. But I'd learned to tell the difference. This was one of those dreams. It meant something. I needed to talk to Colleen.

While I washed my hair, I gave myself a talking to. I had to shake off this funk and get to work. I stepped out of the shower and wrapped up in a towel. "I think I'll eat breakfast at The Cracked Pot this morning."

Nate stood in front of his mirror, shaving. "You got a hankering for country ham and grits?"

"Always. But I want to talk to Blake." I'd feel better if I talked to my brother. He was the police chief of Stella Maris. Evacuations were somewhere in his job description.

"You figure he'd tell you if he knew Sonny was having an affair?"

I startled. How had that not occurred to me? "Never," I said. "The two of them, everything goes into the vault. But I can read my brother like a neon billboard."

"I'm just going to grab something here and head into Charleston quick as I get the paperwork caught up."

"Blake may be more forthcoming if I'm alone. Doubtful, but possible."

After I dressed, I went down to the office and typed up my interview notes from the day before. I wouldn't be right all day if I didn't get that done. Nate worked on his notes in his office, then came by the living room on his way out.

"Are you all right?" He set down his backpack and came over to the desk.

"I'll be fine." I stood, the better to hug him goodbye.

"You're sure looking fine."

"Well, thank you, sir." I'd chosen a black linen jacket and pencil skirt with a polka-dot shell and my Kate Spade black wedge-heel sandals. They were perhaps a bit racy for this book club crowd, with their gold studs on the straps. My toe nail polish offered a pop of pink to the ensemble.

"Don't work too late, hear? Let's get takeout tonight, get you to bed early. You need some rest."

"Sounds good." I looked up and he leaned in to kiss me. It was a sound kiss, one that testified to a deep bond.

"I love you," he said.

I smiled up at him. "I love you too." An ache crept into my heart, echoes of the panic from last night's dream. I couldn't imagine my life without Nate.

*    *    *

As reliable as sunup, my brother walked under the pink striped awning and into The Cracked Pot at eight.

I caught up to him just inside. "Let's get a booth in the back."

He looked me up and down. "You're dressed awful fancy for breakfast here."

Moon Unit Glendawn, the owner of the diner, whose father had an unfortunate fondness for Frank Zappa, breezed out from behind the counter. We'd been friends our entire lives—she'd been one of my bridesmaids. It was a mystery to me why my brother hadn't married her long ago. It was common knowledge she had a crush on him. Moon Unit was a beautiful woman, inside and out. She also manned the control tower for the island's gossip network.

"Good mornin', y'all!" Moon Unit's long, wavy golden hair was pulled back into a ponytail. Her smile, as always, was lit from within.

"Hey, Moon," I said. "Could we have the booth in the back?"

"Sure thing. You both want the usual?" she asked.

"Please." There was no need to verify this with Blake. We both had country ham and grits with red eye gravy, eggs, and biscuits. The only difference in our orders was that I had scrambled eggs with cheese and his eggs were over medium. Always.

"Y'all have a seat. I'll get your coffee." Moon Unit whirled away.

We slid into the corner booth.

"Interesting," I said.

"What?" Blake turned over his coffee cup.

"She didn't even speak to you."

"Sure she did. She said good morning to both of us."

I squinted. "Yeah, but—" Normally she chatted Blake up as much as possible.

Moon Unit approached with the coffee carafe. She filled our cups.

"You doing alright today, Moony?" Blake asked.

She gave him a thin little smile, a far cry from the mega-watt one we'd both received moments ago. "I'm doing fine, Blake. Thank you so much for asking." And she was gone again.

"See?" I said.

Blake grimaced. "Maybe it's her time—"

"*Don't* you even dare." I gave him The Look. The one our mamma had used on all of us our entire lives.

He rolled his eyes. "Did you want to talk to me about something besides Moon Unit's bad mood?"

"She is not in a bad mood. She—" The dream came back to me. The wind. The waves. The people. "Yes. Yes, I did."

He stirred sugar and cream into his coffee, looked at me from under a lowered brow. "What's up with you? You look...shook up."

"I am. This will sound crazy—from nowhere—but we have evacuation procedures, right? For the island? There are plans, I know there are. Town Council has discussed them. To be honest, I didn't focus that much on the specifics. But your department. You monitor these things...storms. It's your job to make sure everyone leaves in time, right?"

"Of course. We have procedures, and we get updates on any threat from the National Hurricane Center. Where is this coming from? There're no storms in the Atlantic."

"It's just on my mind, with all the crazy weather this year. The past couple years, really."

He gave me a look that said he knew that wasn't the whole story.

I said, "But how many people can we evacuate in a day?"

"We typically have more than a day's notice, but if we had to, we could get everyone off the island in twenty-four hours. But you know as well as I do, some folks aren't going to evacuate. Most people here have ridden out a tropical storm or two."

Moon Unit set our plates in front of us. "Y'all enjoy." She turned around and walked away.

"Did you see that?" I said.

"What?"

"When is the last time she brought us food and only said two words? That has never happened. Never."

Blake shrugged. "Are you going to tell me why you're all of a sudden concerned about our evacuation procedures?"

I sighed. "I had a nightmare. A very vivid one. It started me thinking how crazy it is we've all fought against a bridge for years because we love our splendid isolation. People could get hurt—killed, even—if we couldn't get everyone to the mainland."

"Seriously? I know you think you could do my job better than me—"

"That's not true at all."

"Yeah. It is. But nothing about my evacuation plan needs investigating. You just keep on chasing down adulterers and harassing Sonny about his cases. *This* falls under the category of things you don't need to worry about. I worry for all of us.

I've got this."

I watched him for a moment. I knew how much Blake loved this island. "Have you ever thought we ought to cap our population?"

"No. I've never thought that. Are you nuts? Don't answer that. How would you even do that?"

"Ordinances. Hell's bells. I don't know. But I think we need to start figuring out how we avoid reaching the tipping point where we can no longer evacuate everyone in twenty-four hours."

He paused, biscuit halfway to his mouth. "That would sure address development once and for all. You're on the Town Council. Make a motion."

"I need to look into that very thing." I dug into my grits, which had waited far too long for my fork. I savored the thick, creamy, buttery comfort food of my people.

Blake shook his head, muttered something, and sliced off a bite of country ham. We ate in companionable silence for a few moments.

Then I asked, "Do you know if Sonny is seeing anyone?"

Blake seemed to choke just a bit. He washed down whatever he had lodged in his throat with a few gulps of coffee. "Why do you ask?"

"Just curious. I remember him bringing that girl from Folly Beach over to The Pirates' Den a few Fridays ago. She was cute. He seeing anyone else?"

Blake studied his plate.

That was a surefire tell. Something was up.

He said, "You know Sonny."

I did indeed. I also knew my brother.

After we'd finished eating, we took the check to the cash

register. One of the waitresses rang us up. I looked around for Moon Unit. From the window to the kitchen she caught my eye and flashed me a mischievous grin. What game was she playing with Blake? Changing tactics? I hadn't spoken to Moon at any length in a while. Maybe we needed to have lunch.

# EIGHT

I did some of my best thinking on the ferry ride from Stella Maris to Isle of Palms. That particular morning, I was conflicted on several fronts. On the one hand, my training and experience said the smart bet was that Shelby'd had an affair. But I didn't want to believe that.

And because we only had two suspects for the role of Shelby's lover, and one of them had an alibi, that pointed to Sonny. But that went against everything I knew about the man. On the trip into Charleston, I pondered scenarios wherein Charles Kinloch might've had an accomplice to do his dirty work. A rejected lover might resort to cold-blooded murder if he had sociopathic tendencies. But nothing in his background—at least what was on record—hinted at such a thing. I needed to know more about Charles Kinloch.

Once on the peninsula, I headed towards the Kinlochs' home on Huger Street. I'd done some preliminary snooping using Google Street View, and familiarized myself with how the home was situated in the block. There's nothing like a satellite view. I drove past slowly. A two-story frame house, it appeared newish for Charleston. The green wood siding and beige trim looked freshly painted. Flower boxes overflowed on the porch railing. On the wide front porch, deep-cushioned wicker furniture invited you to sit a spell. The house and yard had a spit-shined look to it, like maybe someone had staged it to show.

Jane and Charles Kinloch may have lived in a more modest neighborhood than some of their friends, but they kept things nice. I'd pulled their car registrations Tuesday night. Through the windows in the dark-stained wood garage doors, the tops of both Charles's dark blue Range Rover and Jane's Audi SUV were visible. No way to let myself in and browse through their house for possible motives or evidence of a personality disorder. Damnation.

I had a couple of hours until I had to be at Delta Tisdale's for book club. At the stoplight at Huger and Rutledge I drummed my fingers on the steering wheel. And then I set Charles Kinloch aside for the moment.

I tried calling Paul Baker, but got his voicemail. I didn't leave a message. I zipped on over to the also prescreened West Ashley brick ranch where he and his wife lived with their two kids. Unlike the Kinlochs, the Bakers appeared to've left for the day. Paul's wife worked at a downtown inn. The kids should be at school. Unless something outside the ordinary routine happened, she and the kids wouldn't be home until mid-afternoon at the earliest. The question was, where was Paul?

If he was working a case, he could be anywhere, and be home at any time. He kept an office on Ashley River Road, not much more than a mile from the house, in a strip mall that might've been built in the seventies. I headed in that direction.

The building was brick, but each of the storefronts was painted a different color. Baker's was the washed-out blue one in the middle. His Dodge Caravan—an excellent choice for a PI—was parked in front of the office. I pulled around to the side of the building and parked between two sedans. The side road was narrow and deserted. I popped open the back of the Escape and walked around. My long tan raincoat covered my outfit completely. I pulled my hair up under a ball cap and slid on my largest, darkest sunglasses. Then I retrieved a GPS tracker from the toy box.

I walked around front and strolled down the sidewalk. An awards shop, an empty storefront, Paul Baker Investigations, a Japanese restaurant, a bar, and an office of indeterminate business. A handful of cars were parked out front in the slanted spaces that bordered the sidewalk. But no one was coming or going.

I slipped between Baker's minivan and the SUV parked beside it, faked a stumble just in case I was being observed from inside, caught myself on the side of the Caravan, and slipped the GPS underneath it as I stood.

I smoothed my coat, looked around. Still no company. I walked with a slight limp back to the sidewalk, and slowly made my way back to the end of the building, playing the part all the way to the end of the scene. No one came to see if I was all right. This likely meant no one had seen me "fall."

Back in the Escape, I opened the tracking software on my iPad. The GPS signal was transmitting. I could see the tracker on Baker's van as a dot inside a blue circle on a map. I set the alarm feature to notify me if the van moved, then headed back to the Baker residence. If Paul Baker left the office and came in my direction, I'd know it. I'd also know everywhere else he went.

I parked on the street around the corner. If any of the neighbors happened to be home, they might notice a strange car in the driveway. I scanned the street. It was mid-morning on a weekday. This was a working-class neighborhood. No one was around.

I put my pick set in my pocket, grabbed a kit with a few other toys and slid them along with my iPad into my tote. I walked back to the Baker house. From across the street, I studied the perimeter. It looked to be a three-bedroom, two-bath ranch. Did Baker have the same level of security that we did?

I pulled out my binoculars and scanned for exterior cameras. No sign of any. Several varieties of palm trees and a magnolia screened much of the front of the house, but not enough. Since I'd dressed for the book club meeting, I wasn't disguised enough to go in through the front.

I slipped around back. No exterior cameras here either. But was there a security system inside, and was it armed? I glanced at my iPad to be sure. Baker's van hadn't moved. I pulled a pair of latex gloves from my tote and slipped them on.

I retrieved my pick set from my coat pocket. In less than a minute, I had the deadbolt and the knob lock open. I eased open the back door and entered the kitchen. No tell-tale beeping announced an alarm system that demanded an access code. There were no obvious signs of door sensors, motion detectors, glass breaks, or cameras. Baker could easily have a do-it-yourself system that had none of those things or concealed them well. But his van wasn't moving. If he had any sort of system, I hadn't tripped it. Yet.

I could've spent all day going through Paul Baker's house, but I didn't have that kind of time. He could head home at any moment. He was a PI, and I had to assume, too smart to leave evidence on his computer. And too smart to deposit a large sum of money in a bank account. If he'd taken money to throw the Gerhardt case, he'd likely stashed it somewhere close. Given the apparently unsecured nature of his home, it wasn't likely here. But I had to check.

I went for the closets.

I navigated through the dining area and den and headed down the hall towards the bedrooms. The master was at the end of the hall. I pushed the door open. The bed wasn't made. The room had a cluttered look. I set my iPad on the chest of drawers, glanced at the screen. All clear.

I moved to the closet. The doors were standing open. Many empty hangers mixed in with the hanging clothes. No suitcase in sight. I checked the chest of drawers and dresser. The contents looked thin, like half the clothes were gone.

I went to the other bedrooms. The Bakers had one boy and one girl. Their closets and dressers were likewise low on inventory. I pulled out my iPhone and Googled Planters Inn on North Market. When the results displayed, I tapped the phone icon on the top hit to call.

I asked to speak to Mrs. Baker, said I was calling from the school.

"She's not in this week. They're on vacation. I hope everything's all right with the kids."

"Everything's fine," I said. "I have another contact number. Thank you so much."

The state of the kids' rooms told me that wherever the Bakers had gone, they'd taken the kids along. And they may or may not be coming back in a week. It was odd they'd take the kids out of school for a vacation this close to the end of the year.

Had something spooked Paul and he sent his wife and kids out of town? Or had she left him for one of the standard reasons that had nothing to do with my case? Was he at his office after all, or did he just leave the van there?

I searched the closets more thoroughly. No sign of a bag of cash. The ceilings were the white popcorn stuff blown over sheetrock. No panels to pop up. I pulled the rope to let down the folding attic stairs. Carefully, I climbed the steps, thankful I'd chosen the lower stacked heels.

At the top of the stairs, I pulled the string attached to a light socket. A dim glow revealed a few pieces of plywood flooring with a dozen boxes scattered around. I opened one after the other. Christmas decorations, baby paraphernalia, assorted memorabilia no longer wanted downstairs, but too sentimental to throw away.

The alarm on my iPad sounded.

I scrambled down the rickety stairs, folded them back up, and closed the attic access. Then I dashed back to the master bedroom.

The van was moving. The blue dot was headed in my direction.

I crammed my iPad in my tote and scurried towards the kitchen. I turned the knob lock, closed the door, and dashed back towards the Escape. I climbed in, shut the driver's side door, started the engine, and pulled away. I drove around the block and waited at the stop sign.

Moments later the Dodge Caravan passed the intersection and pulled into the driveway. Paul Baker got out, looked around, scanned the neighborhood. His eyes slipped by the Escape.

Should I confront him? If he'd taken money to look the

other way, he was hardly going to tell me all about it. Better to monitor the GPS, keep an eye on him. And see if his wife and kids came home.

I turned the corner and drove away, pulling off my ball cap and fluffing my hair as I went.

# NINE

I hurried over to Delta Tisdale's charming Colonial Revival mansion on Rutledge Avenue overlooking Colonial Lake. While the house was two blocks north of Broad Street, it was nevertheless no doubt worth a million and a half, maybe more. The double semi-circular porticos and grand columns made the large white house appear even larger. I pegged it at somewhere north of five thousand square feet.

I might've been able to snag a parking spot on the street alongside Colonial Lake, except for the ongoing park improvement project. The landscaping, walkways, and the infrastructure of the lake itself, which was tied via underground pipe to the Ashley River, were all being redone. The entire park was a construction site, fenced for the duration with chain-link, the supports for which sat in what would otherwise be parking spaces.

If things went the way I planned, I would be inside a while. Best not to chance street parking in a residential area without a decal. I made for the closest parking garage at 93 Queen. After I parked, I swapped out my sunglasses and took off my raincoat and left it in the back. It was a short walk back—less than half a mile straight down Queen.

I loitered on the corner of Queen and Rutledge, faked a

phone call for the benefit of child-strollers and dog walkers. I was early on purpose. To say the least, Jane hadn't been enthusiastic about me joining their book club meeting this afternoon. I wanted to catch her on the way in, before Delta or one of the other ladies had a chance to complain to Jane about the intrusion. These were Southern ladies. I knew my people. They would not be ungracious to my face.

I'd considered using a pretext, having Jane claim me as a relative or some such thing. The trouble was that Jane was unaccustomed to lying. At least that was my working theory. In this case, the truth would likely work best. I would be a novelty. These ladies had almost assuredly never met a private investigator.

At eleven forty-five, Jane approached my corner from the same direction I'd come. I ended my imaginary phone call, set Voice Memo to record, and slipped my phone into my inside jacket pocket. I waved to Jane. She waved back, flashed a quick smile.

"Good morning," I called, when she was close enough that I didn't have to shout.

"Good morning. I started to call you several times. I'm not at all sure about this." Jane wore a blue and white print skirt and a sweater set. She carried a copy of *The Prince of Tides.*

"Did you get pushback?"

"Not really. I spoke to Delta. We agreed not to mention it to the others. We're going to introduce you together when everyone gets here. You have to understand. This is highly unusual. None of us know you. Well, I mean, I do, of course. Anyway, it will be easier for both of us if she and I are a united front, so to speak."

I grinned. "So we're going to ambush a group of ladies who lunch."

Jane flushed. "I'm really not comfortable ambushing my friends. But Delta and I both feel that given the circumstances, it's better this way. If we'd told everyone, some of them might've stayed home."

"You're right. That was very smart of y'all." I'd almost asked her to do exactly that, but she'd been so skittish I didn't want to push my luck. "Do you know if everyone is planning to come? You mentioned something yesterday about not everybody showing up to meetings. That was why someone thought their daughter-in-law could join from the wait list?"

"Mary Bernard. Yes. That was her logic for bringing Angela McConnell—her daughter-in-law to be—off the waiting list. But I think everyone is coming today. We've only met twice since Shelby...We took January and February off. March and April we had perfect attendance."

"Shall we go inside?" I asked.

Jane's chest rose and fell with a deep breath. She squared her shoulders. "We might as well."

We crossed Queen Street together and walked up the sidewalk on Rutledge to the wrought iron walk-thru gate. A brick sidewalk led to wide brick steps, which led in turn to the lower portico. Planters at the top of the steps overflowed with large pink blossoms. As we walked up the steps, I noticed that the porch ceiling was painted a soft blue.

"A haint blue porch." I smiled at the tradition. Southerners often painted porch ceilings pale blue to ward off evil spirits.

"You know that doesn't work." Colleen materialized on a wrought iron bench on the porch.

"It's lovely, isn't it?" said Jane. "Wait 'til you see the rest of the house. It was originally built in 1903, but a lot of the woodwork was brought here later from Belvedere Plantation when it was dismantled."

Jane rang the bell to the right of the double white doors.

"I don't know how long I can stay," said Colleen.

*I'm just glad you're here.* I smiled at her.

"You say that now." She grinned.

Colleen had a habit of messing with me, trying to provoke me into talking to her in front of others. It was her favorite game.

*I need to talk to you later.*

The door swung open. A lovely brunette with porcelain skin, dimples, and bright blue eyes stood on the other side. Her deep rose-colored skirt suit complimented her coloring. "Hey, y'all."

"Hey, Delta," said Jane. "This is Liz Talbot. Liz, this is Delta Tisdale."

"So lovely to meet you." I held out a hand. She didn't look like a zombie alien Sasquatch nut.

She took my hand and gave it a ladylike shake. "Oh, it's so nice to meet you too. Come inside. Y'all are the first ones here."

We stepped into the foyer. The house truly was gorgeous. If it was elaborate for my taste, I could still appreciate the ornate woodwork, crystal chandeliers, and antiques. We followed Delta into a living room to the left.

"Please have a seat," Delta said.

A sofa faced the fireplace, above which a gilded mirror rose all the way to the ceiling. Fresh-cut flowers in a crystal vase sat in front of the mirror. Wingbacks flanked the fireplace, and a pair of parson's chairs sat at a right angle to the sofa on each end. Additional chairs, perhaps from the dining room, had been brought in to accommodate the group.

I chose one of the wingbacks by the fireplace. This would give me a good view of the room and the foyer beyond. Also, I liked having my back to the wall. It creeped me out to think of sitting on that sofa with my back to the door.

"I appreciate you agreeing to me joining y'all today," I said to Delta.

"Well, my goodness," she said. "When Jane told me you were looking into Shelby's death, how could I say no? We all loved Shelby. And we know Clint would never have hurt her. The idea is preposterous. I'm just glad someone is working to clear his name. But I confess I am curious how we can help."

"You were Shelby's closest friends. I need to learn as much about her as I can, as fast as I can. And it's possible one of you knows something that you don't realize is helpful to the case."

"Or maybe one of you pushed her out that door in a jealous rage." Colleen popped in and perched on the corner of the massive fireplace mantel. Right above my head.

*This will be a big group. I'm going to have a hard time keeping track. Please don't comment unless you pick up on something I need to know. Please. I'll buy you as many ham biscuits as you like.*

"You'd take every bit of fun out of this if you could," said Colleen. "But I would like some ham biscuits. Fine."

I smiled at Jane and Delta, who'd sat on the sofa across from me.

The doorbell rang and Delta popped up and went to

answer it.

Jane smiled a nervous smile and looked out the window.

We heard Delta make all the same welcoming noises she'd made when we arrived. Then a petite, fifty-ish, blonde woman dressed in a St. John pantsuit entered the room in front of Delta. She carried a copy of *The Prince of Tides*.

Jane and I stood.

Delta said, "Evelyn Izard, please meet Liz Talbot. She's a friend of Jane's. Excuse me. I need to get the door." Delta slipped back into the foyer, though the doorbell hadn't rung.

Jane's eyes doubled in size. Pique and discombobulation danced across her face. The united front method wasn't going to work as well in practice as planned. I couldn't be sure if she was put out with me, Delta, or both of us. She pulled on a welcoming smile, and turned to face Evelyn across the sofa. "Hey, Evelyn. How are you?"

Evelyn Izard. The runner's wife. She was Shelby's neighbor to the right. Her townhouse shared a wall with Clint and Shelby's. Clint had described Evelyn as a lush.

"Well, I'm fine, Jane. How are you?" Evelyn's eyes lighted on me with interest. "Now who did you say this was?"

"I'm Liz Talbot. So lovely to meet you."

Evelyn studied me for a long moment, a small smile on her face. "Are you applying for our waiting list?"

"Oh, no..." I mentally calculated our age difference and decided against adding "ma'am."

Evelyn turned to Jane and lifted her chin, indicating Jane should clarify exactly what I was doing there.

Jane said, "Delta and I thought we should just explain why Liz is here once, after everyone arrives."

"I think that's best," I said. "What a lovely outfit, Mrs.

Izard. That shade of cream is so flattering to you."

"Oh, please. Call me Evelyn. Thank you. I got it on sale at the end of the season. I never pay full price." She commenced rattling on and on about clothes and sales.

I smiled, nodded occasionally.

Evelyn seemed practiced at one-sided conversations.

The doorbell rang again. Presently, Delta escorted a light brown-haired woman into the room. Her St. John pantsuit was navy, and of a slightly different style.

Jane waited for Evelyn to take a breath, then introduced Mariel Camp.

We said our hellos.

Mariel looked at Jane. "Is she here for the waiting list?" Mariel's tone announced her concern regarding the wait list.

Jane assured Mariel I had no interest in joining the book club.

Evelyn picked back up her monologue, but by now she was telling me about her children, who were positively brilliant.

The next three members came in a group, and I had the impression they often traveled that way: Anne Spence, Erin Guidici, and Liz Bell. I pegged them as in their early thirties. Fit, attractive, well-maintained, and all sporting impressive diamond and wedding band sets, these young Charleston matrons appeared to have the world on a string. They said their hellos to Jane and Mariel, smiled politely when introduced to me, then walked on by. They moved to a corner of the room to chat amongst themselves.

Next in was Mary Bernard, a tall, trim woman with shoulder-length brunette hair in a style that had involved curlers. She had Angela McConnell, her soon-to-be daughter-in-law in tow. I remembered from somewhere that Angela was twenty-eight. She was a dark-haired beauty with a sweet smile. Her diamond would compete well with those worn by the group in the corner.

Delta kept delivering new arrivals. Necks were hugged, air-kisses exchanged. Everyone carried a copy of *The Prince of Tides*. Jane waited for an opening in Evelyn's chatter and briefly introduced me to each in turn. Finally, counting me, there were nineteen of us in the room. One by one, I looked at each of the well-dressed women, remembering the names that went with the faces, imprinting it.

Delta stood in the doorway to the foyer. "Y'all, I think everyone is here."

All of the ladies took a seat on cue.

Delta continued, "Welcome everybody to the May 2016 meeting of the Ashley Cooper Book Club. As is our custom, we'll begin with the collect."

I felt my eyes grow. A collect? At book club?

Everyone stood.

"This is different," said Colleen.

It was certainly very, very different from how my own book club meetings started. We opened the wine first thing. My only experience of collects was in church.

All the ladies pulled a small leather-bound notebook from their purses, opened it, and looked up at Delta.

I slid over to look with Evelyn.

In unison, we said:

"Keep us, O God, from pettiness;
let us be large in thought, in word, in deed.

Let us be done with fault-finding and
leave off self-seeking.

May we put away all pretense and meet each
other face to face—without self-pity
and without prejudice.

May we never be hasty in judgment and
always generous.

Let us take time for all things;
make us to grow calm, serene, gentle.

Teach us to put into action our better impulses,
straightforward and unafraid.

Grant that we may realize it is the little
things that create differences,
that in the big things of life we are at one.

And may we strive to touch and to know the great,
common human heart of us all, and
O Lord God, let us forget not to be kind!"

The collect was attributed to Mary Stewart, and titled
simply "A Collect for Club Women." What a lovely sentiment.

"They use that in Women's Clubs—service clubs—all
over," said Colleen.

*How do you know that?*

"You know that thing you use to look stuff up on the
computer?"

*Google?*

"Whatever. I have something like it in my head now."

Everyone closed their books and sat down. I slipped back over to my chair, smoothed my skirt, and sat.

Delta said, "We'll head into the dining room in just a moment. Francina has a lovely luncheon prepared for us. Everyone knows Angela, who is here today as Mary's guest."

Angela smiled, gave a little wave.

Delta continued, "I think you've all been introduced to Liz Talbot, our other guest. Liz, would you stand, please, and tell everyone a little about yourself? Perhaps you'll have a chance to speak to some of the members individually during lunch."

I grabbed a small stack of business cards from my purse and stood. Neither Jane nor Delta would make eye contact. Delta sat down, ceding me the floor. So be it.

They all looked at me with polite curiosity.

"Good morning. As Delta mentioned, I'm Liz Talbot. I'm a private investigator, hired by Clint Gerhardt's attorneys to assist in his defense. I know many of you were close to Shelby. I'm hoping to learn as much about her as possible. And I hope to discover if one or more of you has information important to the investigation that perhaps you don't realize is important. I'd love to talk with each of you today. But I'm going to pass around my business cards. If you think of something later, please call me."

The nature of their gazes changed gradually as I spoke. By the time I'd finished, some were exchanging glances with each other. Others regarded me with avid interest.

Delta said, "Y'all please share with Liz anything that might be related, even if you don't think it's important. We of course want her to get to the bottom of what happened to our Shelby. Now, let's have some lunch, and then we'll have our business meeting, followed by our discussion of *The Prince of Tides.*"

Business meeting? What kind of business did book clubs have? The membership issues, but Clint mentioned something about a treasurer. What were these ladies up to that they needed a treasurer?

Delta made her way through the room and opened a set of pocket doors that revealed the dining room. She stepped back, inviting everyone to go in front of her. "There are tables set up on the side porch and in the front parlor. Please sit anywhere you like."

We all stood, left our things at our chairs, and filed towards the dining room. The decor was similar to the foyer and the living room—intricate, white-painted woodwork, crystal chandelier, expensive-looking rug over gleaming wood floors.

I meandered towards Delta, who stood at the doorway to the dining room.

"I wanted to ask you about something," I said. "Perhaps after we get our lunch we can find a quiet corner?"

"Of course." Her eyes didn't express the same enthusiasm her voice did.

Slowly, the line moved along. As the ladies filled their plates and selected from urns of water infused with cucumber and mint and several varieties of tea, they made their way out of the dining room.

I waited to take the next-to-last place in line, in front of the hostess. The spread of food on the table and sideboard was a work of art. A variety of small sandwiches, salads, spreads, cheeses, fruit, cakes, tarts—this looked like something my mamma had done. My mouth watered.

"This food looks fabulous," I said.

"Francina is a wonder."

I picked up a china plate from the stack and selected food strategically. I was a guest, and needed to resist the urge to pile it full. I splurged on the peach tea, then waited for Delta. As we left the dining room, something in my peripheral vision caught my eye. I glanced over my shoulder to see Colleen, who had solidified in a kelly green shirtdress, fixing a plate.

*Hell's bells, Colleen. What are you thinking? Behave.* I threw the thought over my shoulder.

"I'm starving," she said. "They have ham biscuits—did you get one? No one will see me. Everyone's busy eating."

*If someone does, I don't have the first clue who you are.*

"I'll tell them I'm here about that waiting list."

Delta led me through the foyer into the parlor. Two ladies sat at one of three skirted tables. Otherwise, the room was empty.

"Most everyone's on the porch," said Delta. "Let's sit back here." She nodded towards the table on the far side of the room.

I took the back chair, facing the room. After we'd settled in and tasted a few bites, I said, "Clint told me Shelby was working on book club business in her library the night she was killed. You're president now. What kinds of things would she have been doing?"

"In December, she would likely have been typing up the list of books we'd decided on for the new year, and where we were going to purchase them. Since we never got it, I assume that's what she was working on."

"So you choose your books a year in advance."

"That's right. We have a meeting and everyone makes suggestions. We discuss them and take a vote."

"What did you mean by 'where you were going to purchase them?'" I asked.

"Well, we generally try to support independent book stores. Each of us adopts one of the SIBA stores—that's Southern Independent Booksellers Alliance—and for that year we order our books from that store. This year I'm ordering from Quail Ridge Books and Music in Raleigh."

"Was there anything controversial about the books or stores? Anything anyone might've been upset about?"

"No, not at all. The only controversy we have is over the waiting list." She sighed heavily, moved food around on her plate. "That's going to be an ugly mess. I had hoped not to deal with it today. But with Shelby gone, someone moves off the wait list and joins the club. I've put off dealing with this as long as I can. Mary wants that person to be Angela, and of course she's here, which makes it awkward."

"Angela's not at the top of the list, is she?"

"No." Delta shook her head. "That's Mariel's friend, Nerissa Long. She's sweet as sugar and has been waiting years. But she's heartbroken that she's taking Shelby's place. She offered to give her spot to Angela just to avoid taking Shelby's spot. And of course she knows about the controversy. But we just can't do that."

"Why not, if that's what Nerissa wants?"

Delta sipped her tea. "Because Nerissa will be our first black member. I will not have our club even appear to be anything less than welcoming to Nerissa."

"Does that bother anyone?" I asked.

"You mean that she's black? No, of course not. We're all friends with Nerissa. But if we skip over her, even at her request, some people would see it as racist."

"Just to be clear, before there was an opening—when Shelby planned to bring it to a vote to allow Angela to come off the waiting list—Shelby wasn't in favor of skipping over Nerissa, was she?"

"Oh my goodness, no. Shelby would never have allowed that. She agreed to entertain a motion from Mary to allow the next two people on the waiting list, Nerissa and Angela to join the club. Someone would've had to have seconded the motion, and then there would've been a vote."

"You said Nerissa has been on the waiting list for years."

"That's right."

"How long has Angela been on it?"

"About as long—several years."

"So she was on the waiting list for the club before she was engaged to Mary Bernard's son?"

"Oh my, yes, long before that."

"Then this isn't something she's doing to please her future mother-in-law?"

"No, no."

"And you're not going to have a vote on letting Angela join as well?"

"No. I know that's what Shelby had planned. I loved Shelby, but I didn't agree with her on this. Our book club is more than a hundred years old. Several of our great-grandmothers started it. We have traditions. If we start changing things, some people will like some of the things, but others won't. There will be drama. The only way to keep us from quarreling is to leave things as they are."

"But won't there be a quarrel about that?" I asked.

"Mary won't agree with it, but as long as we don't change anything else, she'll let it go. I hope. Shelby was more open to change than most of our members. Mary knew that, and I personally think she was taking advantage of her. I'm just trying to keep the peace and do the right thing."

"I wish you luck with that," I said. "If it had come to a vote, would Mary have gotten her way?"

Delta raised both shoulders. "Who knows? Mary has friends who she may have persuaded to vote her way. Or it may have just ended up embarrassing poor Angela because it didn't pass. It's better to just leave things as they are."

I said, "Your book club is fascinating. I confess I've never been to one quite like it. I'm very impressed. Someone mentioned you have a treasurer. Do you all pay dues?"

"We do, and we have quarterly fundraisers. Usually it's a wine auction or a vacation raffle—something like that. We donate the money to various groups that support literacy."

"What a fabulous idea. You all are very industrious. Have you had any issues with the money—who to give it to, some going missing—anything like that?" Money was a reliable troublemaker.

"Never."

I took a bite of a cucumber sandwich. We ate for a few minutes, and then I said, "There's one other thing I wanted to ask you about. I understand you mentioned to the previous investigators that Shelby spoke a lot about Sonny Ravenel. Do you have any ideas as to the nature of their relationship?"

Delta's cheeks went pink. "All I know is that Shelby mentioned his name often. She'd repeat things he said—

funny things. Sometimes she'd tell me stories about how he'd helped someone. I know they both volunteered at One80Place. That was Shelby's favorite charity. I guess that gave them a lot in common."

"Do you think there was more to their relationship than a common interest?" I asked.

"I don't know." Delta's voice held frustration and despair. "If I did know, I would tell you. Shelby was very private. I can tell you they had lunch together regularly. She admired him. Beyond that, I have no idea."

"Did she talk about Sonny as much as she talked about Clint?"

Delta's brow wrinkled. "No, not at all. Shelby talked about Clint all the time. My impression is that she loved him very much."

"So you didn't suggest to Paul Baker that Shelby was having an affair with Sonny?"

"Good Heavens, no. I would never imply such a thing. That pesky vulgarian kept at me until I came up with the name of a man Shelby knew. I probably shouldn't have said anything."

Interesting. Had Baker stretched what Delta said to justify chasing the affair theory?

"One more thing, Delta," I said. "Please don't take offense, but for my files, I need to check everyone off. Where were you the night Shelby died?"

"Me?" Delta leaned back and blinked. "Why, I was here at home with my boys."

"Oh, you have children. How old are they?"

"Fourteen and fifteen."

"How nice to have family time over the holidays. I hope

your husband didn't have to travel like poor Jane's."

Delta flushed. "My former husband's affairs are no concern of mine."

"I'm terribly sorry. I didn't know." I would've found out, given another day to research all these people.

"Don't give it a thought. How would you have known?"

I smiled a small sheepish smile.

Erin Guidici entered the room, scanned it with her eyes, then approached our table. "Excuse me, y'all. Liz, could I have a word with you in private?"

"Certainly." I looked at Delta. "I'll be right back."

I followed Erin through the foyer, up three steps to a landing, then up a half-flight of stairs to a second landing. Anne and the other Liz waited there.

I joined their huddle.

Erin said, "We hate to mention this. It could be nothing."

Anne looked doubtful. "It's not nothing."

"Just tell her," said the other Liz.

Erin said, "There was something going on between Angela McConnell and Shelby."

I scrunched my face at her. "What do you mean?"

"Well, you know," Anne said. "Angela is dying to join book club. And I guess she wanted to talk to Shelby about it. We had book club at Shelby's house in December, in the evening. That was our tradition. Shelby loved Christmas, and she loved having lots of candlelight."

"Most everyone had left," said Liz. "We were saying goodbye to the dogs and Belly—she's a potbellied pig. They were in the guest room up on the third floor. Jane told us later that as she was leaving, Angela came by and asked to speak with Shelby privately. We'd already gone upstairs at that point."

Erin and Anne looked at Liz, as if to encourage her to finish the story.

Liz threw up both hands, fingers spread. "When we were coming back down to the second floor, we overheard Angela and Shelby arguing in the library. We stopped on the stairs."

"What were they arguing about?" I asked.

The other Liz said, "We couldn't make out what they were saying at first. Then we heard Shelby say, 'How could you?' She sounded real hurt. Maybe crying."

Anne jumped in. "Then Angela said, 'No one has to know your dirty little secret. How, and with *who*, you've been spending your afternoons. My, my, Shelby Poinsett. What would people say?' Her voice was all hateful. She was taunting Shelby."

Erin said, "And then she said, 'All you have to do is bring this thing to a vote. And, naturally, vote in favor of letting me in. Convince the others it's the right thing to do. Like I said, no one has to know. It's all in your hands.'"

Damnation. Definitely blackmail. An affair. Please don't let it be Sonny.

Erin said, "Then Angela came stalking out of the room, ran down the steps, and blew out the front door. She never even looked our way."

Anne said, "We slipped back up the stairs into the guest room with the pets. We didn't want to embarrass Shelby by letting on we'd overheard. After a few minutes we came back out and said bye to her. We could tell something was wrong, but of course we didn't mention anything."

"Have y'all reported this to anyone else?" I asked.

"No," Erin said. "It seemed like...you know, just book

club drama. Nothing that the police would be interested in. And no one's ever asked us a thing."

The other Liz said, "But since you're here, and you did say we might know something but not realize it was important...We talked about it and decided you should determine if it was important or not."

"Think hard," I said. "Was that everything you heard?"

"Yes," said the other Liz. "We've gone over it several times."

"Thank you for telling me," I said. "It might not be related to Shelby's death. But on the other hand, it could be. If you think of anything else, please call me."

"I just feel so relieved," said Erin.

"You did the right thing," I said. "Hey, where were y'all on December 28—the night Shelby was killed? I have to document where all her friends were."

Erin spoke for the group. "We were all at my house, having a dinner party. Our husbands were there, and two other couples. Would you like their names?" Her tone let me know she offered as a formality and fully expected me to say that wouldn't be necessary.

"That'd be great, thanks." I offered her my sunniest smile.

She rattled off a couple of mister and missuses.

"Would you text me those names and phone numbers, please? Thank you so much. I need to get back downstairs."

I was on the first landing when I heard the sound of glass breaking.

"Oh, Lord Jesus, save me!" The cry came from the back of the house.

I darted into the dining room, then stepped through the

door to the left of the fireplace into the kitchen.

A black woman in khakis and a polo shirt, with an elaborate hairdo made up of baby dreads, was backed up against the oversized refrigerator. Broken china littered the tile floor around her. Her eyes were large with fright.

Colleen was on the other side of the island. She'd morphed back to where only I could see her. I assumed the plate and glass on the counter were hers.

"You must be Francina," I said.

The lady in front of the refrigerator nodded.

"Is everything all right?" I asked.

She shook her head vigorously.

Colleen said, "I slipped in here to eat. When she came in from the hallway, I dematerialized. But I didn't set my plate and glass down quite fast enough. I didn't mean to scare her."

Delta burst into the room, follow by Jane, and as many of the other ladies as would fit. "Francina, what's wrong?"

"I went out to clear the dishes on the porch. I came back in with a stack of plates, and...I know this sounds crazy, but that plate and glass on the island? They were floating in the air, like someone was holding them. And then they just floated onto the island, all by themselves. I'm so sorry about your beautiful china. I'll replace it."

"Don't be silly," said Delta. "Have you had your lunch yet?"

"No, not yet."

"I bet your blood sugar's dropped. Here, sit down and let me fix you a plate." She led Francina to the kitchen table.

Francina kept staring at the plate on the island.

Delta raised her voice. "Everything's fine. Everyone please go back to the living room. I'll be right in."

Slowly, with a lack of enthusiasm, the ladies evacuated the kitchen.

I hung back.

Colleen said, "I don't want Delta to not believe her. And I don't want that poor woman to feel like she needs to replace all that expensive china."

*What are you planning to—*

Colleen picked up the plate and glass.

Francina pointed.

Delta turned to look.

She gasped and her eyes went wide. "What in this world?"

"Delta," I said, "it's possible you have a ghost in the house. But it seems like a harmless one, if a bit mischievous."

"Shelby?" said Delta.

"Oh Lord Jesus," said Francina. "Is that you, Miss Shelby?"

"It could be," I said. "Have you ever had anything like this happen before?"

"Never," said Delta.

Colleen set the dish and glass on the counter.

Delta and Francina gasped and jumped a little.

"I wonder if she's trying to tell us something," said Delta.

"If only she could," I said.

*Colleen, I'm going to leave. Sit in on the meeting. Stay as long as you can, and tell me what they talk about after I'm gone.*

"I guess I owe you that much," said Colleen.

Delta said, "I need to get back to the meeting. Francina, go on up to the front guest room. I'll fix you a plate and bring it up."

"Thank you. I'd appreciate that." Francina backed out of the room.

"Why don't you let me fix her a plate?" I said. "I'll take it up and just slip out after I get her settled. I think I have what I need."

"That's probably for the best," said Delta. "The business meeting is next, and we don't need to air our dirty laundry in front of you. Thank you for taking care of Francina."

"My pleasure."

Delta headed towards the pass-through to the dining room.

*Colleen...*

"I'm on it."

I piled Francina's plate high and took it upstairs with a glass of the peach tea. She seemed to be recovering. She'd quickly attached to the idea that the ghost was Shelby. She knew Shelby meant her no harm.

"Thank you, Miss Liz," she said.

"My pleasure. Can I get you anything else?"

"No ma'am. I'll be fine."

"All right then. Bye now." I stepped out of the guest room and pulled the door closed. This was a golden opportunity to snoop. See if Delta was the genteel lady she seemed to be, or perhaps the mean-spirited zombie-alien-Sasquatch crazy I'd first suspected her of being.

Just as the door clicked shut, Francina called out. "Miss Liz?"

I opened the door. "Yes, Francina. What is it?"

"Would you please leave the door open? Just in case..."

"Of course."

Damnation.

I smiled. "Is there a powder room on this floor?"

"No ma'am. But there's one downstairs just off the hall."

"Thanks." The way the room was situated, Francina would see if I did anything but go back downstairs. Reluctantly, I moved towards the steps. I smiled and waved as I descended.

Francina waved back, smiling.

When I made it to the first landing, I could hear the minutes from the last meeting being read. Hell fire. I was going to have to go back into the room and get my purse. I padded towards the living room. Then I noticed my purse on the round table in the center of the foyer. Delta must've set it there for me. I picked it up and cast a glance into the living room as I walked by.

Colleen was on the job. She'd returned to her perch on the mantel.

I let myself out the front door and made my way back to the parking garage. As I set my purse on the passenger seat, I noticed a folded piece of ivory paper in the outside pocket.

I slipped it out and unfolded it. The unsigned note said, "It's possible Delta has a crush on Clint Gerhardt."

And just like that, we had one more potential motive.

In sorting through the web of possible motives friends, family, and fond acquaintances might've had to kill Shelby, we'd somehow failed to consider what should've been obvious.

Clint was a handsome, wealthy man.

With Shelby out of the picture, he was a handsome, wealth, available man.

# TEN

Tallulah Poinsett had agreed to speak to me at three. I had some time to kill, so I cruised East Battery, Water, Meeting, and South Battery with the moonroof open until a parking spot opened up on East Battery. Charleston was dressed in her prettiest spring frock—colorful blooms burst from planters, beds, and bushes. Deep green palm fronds danced against the bright blue sky. I parked and rolled the windows down.

I tried calling Sonny. He was apparently avoiding me. I left him another message and beat down my anxiety. I knew Sonny. If Shelby'd had an affair—and whether I liked it or not, it was looking more like she had—it wasn't with him.

I pulled my iPad out to check on Paul Baker. He had changed locations—or at least his van had. The map on my GPS locator screen had him at a spot on a back corner of Oak Plantation Campground, about seven miles down Savannah Highway from his house. Was he working a case, or hiding out? He surely wasn't vacationing that close to home. Was that where his wife and kids were?

I mulled the note someone—who?—had left in my purse. Delta, from all appearances, was a proper Southern lady, not a zombie alien Sasquatch loon after all. Divorce had become so commonplace it wouldn't diminish her reputation in the slightest. Would she covet her friend's husband? And if she did, was it an innocent crush she'd never act on? Or was it one of those boil the rabbit scenarios from *Fatal Attraction*? Maybe Colleen would pick up on something, spend some time browsing Delta's mind.

I opened the Numbers app on my iPad and created a spreadsheet with a list of all the book club members, my initial impressions of each, and the alibis I'd gathered already. Being at home with your kids was not a particularly strong alibi. That said, I wasn't keen on questioning the children to verify their mothers' alibis. I'd leave that as a last resort. With a couple of quick phone calls, I verified Erin, Anne, and the other Liz's whereabouts on the night Shelby died. Unless there was a conspiracy—too unlikely to spend time on at this point—they were all in the clear.

At three o'clock, I got out of the car and crossed the street to the Poinsett home. It was a lovely three-story, rosy-taupe colored masonry structure with stacked side verandahs and a front balcony with lacy wrought iron railing. I passed through the street-level gate and took the sidewalk to the door at the front of the house. I rang the bell and waited. Presently, a woman opened the door.

"Ms. Talbot?" she asked.

"Yes. Thank you for seeing me, Mrs. Poinsett." This beautiful creature could only be Shelby's mother. The resemblance was striking, though time and grief had lined Tallulah Poinsett's face. She wore her muted blonde hair in a bob. Her soft knit outfit might've come from J. Jill. While neat and attractive, nothing about her personal appearance screamed *I have tons of money.*

"Of course. Please come in." She led me down the hall and up the stairs to the second floor. The home could've been a museum. Built in the early 1800s, like several of its neighbors it had withstood the Civil War, the Earthquake of 1886, and countless hurricanes. The decor, though doubtless expensive, was tasteful and elegant.

"Let's talk on the verandah, shall we?" she said. "I've brought us out some iced tea."

I followed her and we settled into a deeply cushioned wrought iron conversation area, me on the sofa, her in a chair. She poured us each a glass of tea, then picked hers up and slid back in her chair.

"Forgive Williams for not being here," she said. "He just can't talk about Shelby without breaking down. It's still too fresh. Although, I honestly can't imagine this ever getting easier. They say it's the worst. Losing a child. I believe that's true."

My eyes watered. "Mrs. Poinsett..." I swallowed hard. "I had hoped not to trouble you. I truly am sorry."

"Nonsense. If I can help in any way, I want to. I know in my heart that Clint didn't hurt Shelby. I want whoever did to pay dearly."

I nodded. "First, is there anything you can think of that you'd want me to know?"

"Just what I've told you. Clint is innocent. He's like mine, you understand? He's part of our family—one of us. Clint knew the value of family because he had such a horrible one when he was a child. He treasured Shelby."

"I understand—I do. I hope you understand why I have to ask a few questions that will sound like I suspect him. I don't. I've met Clint. I want to help him, and in fact that's what I was hired to do. But because so often the love of money is at the root of violence, I need to ask the hard questions."

"Very well."

"I understand Shelby's trust was redone when she and Clint married."

"That's right. That's what Shelby wanted. She never wanted money to be an issue between them. She said she wanted it to all be as much his as hers. Williams and I had thoroughly vetted Clint. We saw no reason not to do as Shelby asked."

"So if they ever divorced, he would've gotten half of everything that was hers?"

"Well, it wasn't hers anymore. At least not only hers. So, yes. Half would've been his. It already was."

"And jointly, their approximate net worth was..."

"Approximately two hundred and fifty million."

I gulped several times, cleared my throat. "And now it's all his."

"Well, yes," she said. "But half of that would've been a great deal of money. Even if I thought him capable of such a thing, it's not reasonable that he killed her for the money."

"I agree. Is there anyone else who benefitted financially in any way from her death?" I'd asked this question to both Clint and Jane. But with that much money involved, I needed verification.

"No. Williams and I have seen families devour themselves over money. We took steps to prevent that from happening to ours."

I nodded, sipped my tea. "Were you aware of anyone Shelby was having problems with?"

"Not at all. Shelby was the kind of person who made peace with people. She always looked for ways to solve problems. She's just the last person in the world you'd think anyone would want to hurt." Her voice cracked and a tear slipped down her face.

"I've heard several people say similar things—what a warm, tender-hearted person she was. I promise you, I'm going to do everything I can to find out who did this."

She composed herself, took a few sips of tea. "I beg your pardon."

"No, ma'am. I beg yours for stirring all this up."

"It's not like it ever goes away."

I swallowed hard, took a deep breath. "Do you know of anyone in Shelby's circle—friends, family—who you would say is maybe mercurial? Someone who might not've intended to hurt Shelby, but who maybe became overwrought?"

She sighed, stared out into the garden for a moment. "I dislike gossip. I never engage in it, nor did Shelby. But if I'm honest, I have to tell you that Delta Tisdale has always struggled with her emotions. At times I've wondered if she might be bipolar. Most of the time she's sweet as sugar. But once in a while...I believe if you checked her bathroom cabinet, you might find she's medicated. Ask her former husband, Tommy. I can't imagine a scenario where she would turn on Shelby. But that doesn't mean it couldn't have happened."

Oh, sweet reason. I knew I needed to poke around more at Delta's house. If only Francina hadn't been upstairs, I could've slipped up and taken my time while the business meeting and book discussion took place downstairs.

"No ma'am," I said. "It doesn't. I'll follow up on that,

thank you. I need to ask you to take a look at something."

"All right."

"I have Shelby's address book here." I pulled it from my purse. "I know Lark Littleton was her college roommate. And I think I know most of her local friends, but there are a few names I can't identify. Could you take a look and tell me who these folks are? I've marked them with sticky notes." I handed her the notebook.

"Shelby hasn't spoken to Lark in years. They exchange Christmas cards, that sort of thing. Lark and her husband own a very successful restaurant in San Francisco. She's busy with her life. Shelby stayed busy too." She flipped through the pages. "All of these girls you have marked went to college with Shelby. She hasn't stayed in touch with them. Like Lark—the occasional card, and even those have dwindled. I can't imagine any of them have anything to do with this."

"That's the trouble with this case."

"What do you mean?" She handed me the address book back.

"There are no good suspects. No one can imagine anyone wanting to hurt Shelby. And because of the situation—with her and Clint locked inside the house—the person who killed her must have been someone she trusted enough to let in the house. But that doesn't necessarily mean someone close to her. Just someone she wasn't afraid of. There's quite a long list to work through."

"I see your problem. I can eliminate a few people for you."

"Really? How?"

"We were invited to a dinner party that evening. It was an informal thing, some of the folks from church. Williams and I didn't go because I wasn't well. If you need to check on us, I don't know what to tell you. But the dinner party was at Mary and Jack Bernard's house."

"Mary Bernard who's in Shelby's book club?"

"Yes. And Mariel and Roy Camp were there. The Wilkinsons and the Butlers as well. Though honestly, I wouldn't think any of the folks from church would be suspects. But that should help you cross a few names off your list. Mary can confirm all that, of course."

"Of course. Thank you. This is helpful." Thank Heavens I could erase a few names from our case board. After I verified they were all actually present at the Bernard residence. "So there was nothing controversial going on at the church? I know that sounds crazy, but I wouldn't've thought the book club ladies would have so much drama either."

"Oh, you mean that waiting list kerfuffle? Goodness gracious, that was nothing anyone would hurt anybody over. And no, nothing remotely like that was going on at our church. It's a very special place."

"Thank you, Mrs. Poinsett. You've been very helpful. If I have any further questions, is it all right if I call you?" I rose to leave.

She stood. "Certainly. Call me any time. I mean that. It would do me good to help."

"Oh, one more quick thing," I said.

She looked at me expectantly.

"Do you recall Shelby ever mentioning the name Sonny Ravenel?" I asked.

"The police detective who volunteers with her?"

"That's right."

"She talked about him all the time. Sounds like a nice

fellow. You don't suspect he killed my Shelby, do you?"

"No ma'am. I'm just checking off my list."

The stop sign just inside the entrance at Oak Plantation Campground insisted all visitors must register at the office. But since there was no one around to notice whether I did or not, I saved myself the time it would take to come up with and deliver a story and drove on in.

I've never spent time at a campground, so I had nothing to compare this one to. But it looked inviting, well-organized. An asphalt road led down the center, with two sections of grassy campsites laid out on grids with a nice shade canopy. Massive motorhomes, travel trailers, and the occasional pop-up camper were scattered throughout the grounds. There wasn't a tent in site.

Two rows back from where the GPS indicated Baker's van was still parked, I pulled over to an empty site between two deserted-looking motorhomes. Likely, the occupants were downtown sightseeing or at the beach. I grabbed shorts, a knit top, tennis shoes, and socks from a duffle in the back, slipped into the backseat, and executed a wardrobe change with a high difficulty score. Then I put my ball cap and large sunglasses back on and went for a stroll.

I smiled and waved at folks sitting around campsites. I was just another camper out for a walk on a pretty day. Every once in a while, I stopped to take pictures of trees, birds, other nature. Unlike the other sections of the campground, the access roads running off the main road here ended in cul-de-sacs. There were no campsites along the far side, and thus no loop. I walked to the end of the row I'd parked on, turned around and walked back to the main road, turned left, and headed to the back row. Gradually, I made my way to the back left corner spot.

Part of me worried Baker had found the GPS, left it on another vehicle for me to find, and this was a fine goose chase. But as I neared the end of the cul-de-sac, his van came into view. It was partially hidden, parked between the tree line and a shiny silver Airstream trailer. Also on the site was a diesel Ford F-350, which was likely used to tow the trailer. It had been backed into the site, so the tag wasn't visible.

Was this his trailer? His truck? I hadn't run across it when I'd pulled the Caravan registration and his wife's Camry. But I'd been in a hurry.

No sign of Baker. No sign of anyone. I did a one-eighty at the end of the drive, made a show of checking my watch, which did not count steps, but no one watching knew that. I made my way back to the Escape. Baker had already seen it once today. I didn't want to get close enough for him to spot it. But I needed to get closer to have a view of the site.

A burgundy motor coach was parked across the street from Baker. I could see it from where I was parked. It was on the row between mine and his. I pulled out my binoculars. No one appeared to be at home. It was possible someone was inside, but there was no car parked beside the motorhome and no signs of life.

I put my iPad in my tote and walked over to knock on the door. No answer. I perused the campsite. A group of chairs were set up around a fire pit. I chose one facing Baker's campsite. Then I opened my iPad, logged onto one of our subscription databases, and rechecked for vehicles registered to Paul Baker or his wife. Neither the trailer nor the truck were there. I cross-checked with a property database that referenced tax info. Nothing.

Had Baker created some sort of corporation to own the truck and trailer, or did they belong to someone else, a friend maybe? If I was into something shady—like taking money to double-cross Fraser Rutledge on a murder case—I might plan for the possibility of having to disappear. That trailer was certainly big enough for the whole family. I'd wait for a while. Maybe he'd leave in the van. Then I could get the tag numbers easy enough, see where they led.

It was almost five o'clock when Baker approached on foot, alone, with a fishing rod. I'd passed a lake on the way in. I made him at under six feet tall, but not by much. In his mid-forties, he carried extra weight around the middle and had a receding hairline. He wore khaki shorts and a t-shirt and blended in well with the other campers I'd seen. His head slowly swiveled, scanning in all directions. This was the trouble with investigating investigators. It was impossible to tell if he was here surveilling someone else, or making himself scarce in case someone came looking for him.

No one came out to greet him. He put the fishing rod in the back of the truck and unlocked the trailer door. Had anyone been inside, at a campground, I doubted the door would've been locked. He didn't call out a greeting.

From behind me, a car approached.

Shit.

I stood, turned, and waved enthusiastically.

A family of four, Mom, Dad, and two preteen kids, got out of a Jeep Wrangler.

I plastered a surprised, ditzy blonde smile on my face. "Well, y'all aren't Aunt Jean and Uncle Buster."

"No, honey, I'm afraid we're not," said the mom.

I raised my hands to my cheeks in embarrassment. "I am so sorry. They were supposed to get in today, and their camper looks just like y'all's. I've been sitting here just waiting for them. I figured they'd gone over to the Publix to get groceries."

"No problem," said the dad. "We won't even charge a chair rental. Maybe you should check at the office and see which spot they're in."

"Oh. That's what I should've done to start with. Y'all excuse me. I am just mortified to death." I moved past them, towards my car.

"Hope you find your family," the mom called out.

"Thank you," I called over my shoulder. "Bye."

# ELEVEN

Colleen took the ferry ride back to Stella Maris with me. We sat on the upper deck to drink in the sunshine and salt air. I had my earbuds in so folks would assume I was on a phone call and not on the run from the nervous hospital.

"So fill me in. What did I miss at the business meeting and book discussion?" I said.

"The minutes from the last meeting, the treasurer's report. Delta reminding everyone they're reading *To Kill a Mockingbird* next month. The theme for the year is southern classics. After that, there was a very ladylike cat fight over that waiting list."

"Do tell?"

"Delta announced that Nerissa Long would be joining the club at the next meeting, pursuant to the well-established bylaws."

"I bet Mary Bernard wasn't one bit happy."

"Boy howdy. She tried to raise the issue of voting on letting Angela join as well, but Delta held her ground. She said the bylaws just wouldn't permit it, and she was very sorry, but Angela was next up, and she hoped she would be joining soon. Then Mary asked her if she was expecting any more sudden vacancies."

"She didn't."

"Yes, she did. There was a very tense back and forth between them. I'm giving you the Cliff's Notes version."

"How did the other women respond?"

"They all just sat there, staring. No one wanted in the middle of that."

"Could you get inside any of their heads?" I asked. "Delta's?"

"Her mind was occupied with the business at hand."

"How about anyone else?"

"That Evelyn Izard is a piece of work. Of course she was riveted like the rest of them during the unpleasantness. I'd wager she's a talker—this will get out. Probably already has. Before that, though—during the minutes. Her head was a scramble of arranging her children's lives—I think they must be adults seeing as how she was wantin' grandbabies—critiquing everyone's outfits, who's gained weight—Delta has put on a few pounds, in case you're interested—wondering if Delta's off her meds, and planning cocktail hour. She's looking forward to that."

"Any idea what kind of meds Delta's on?" I asked.

"Nah. I thought maybe it was something to help her lose weight, since Evelyn went straight from her weight to wondering if she's off her meds. But there may not be a connection. Like I said, Evelyn's head was a scramble. Oh, and here's a fun fact I picked up from Mariel Camp, who thinks Evelyn is a scatterbrained lush. Evelyn's husband is having an affair with a woman his daughter's age."

"Ewww. Probably why he's decked out in the best running gear. He's got to stay fit for his sweet young thing. Anything else related to who killed Shelby?"

"I was able to get a peek inside Jane's head."

"And?"

"She was a nervous wreck during the tussle. She purely hates drama. She wished Delta would just give Mary her way and move on. On the other hand, she was also nervous Delta might make a scene if Mary didn't let it go. But before all that started was the most interesting thing."

"Colleen. Don't leave me hanging. What?"

"Jane just kept giving all these women little side glances, wondering if you could possibly be on to something. Could any of them have killed Shelby? She was all wound up about that."

"Interesting," I said. "That means I can mark her off the possible suspects list." And not have to question her children, thank Heaven.

"You're welcome." Colleen wore her smug look.

"Good job. Seriously. I appreciate it."

"I'm sorry about the thing with Francina. I feel really bad about that. I shouldn't've materialized. It's just...as wonderful as it is where I am, sometimes I regret checking out early. I missed a lot. I've never been to a fancy lunch like that. And I know all that's so trivial in the big picture. But sometimes..."

My eyes misted over. "I've missed having you around for so many things. I regret every day not being there for you like I should've been. I hate that you felt that alone, that desperate."

"It wasn't your fault. It was my choice and mine alone."

"But would you've made that choice if I'd been a better friend?"

"You can't carry that burden. We each write the story of our lives one choice at a time. Sometimes those choices are terminal."

We sat in silence with our regrets for a few moments. Then I said, "I had a nightmare last night."

"I know."

"Is that real? Is that our future?"

Colleen sighed. "Mortals have free will, and not all of them are on the side of the angels. The future is constantly changing based on decisions people make every day. Take Shelby for example. Because of one person's actions, things changed for so many people when Shelby died. Her family, of course, but also all the lives she would've touched if she'd lived. Sonya and Kelly...countless others."

"Shelby's death was tragic for way more people than just her family."

After a minute, Colleen said, "The painter who cut his ear off? Van Gogh...he was an Impressionist—that's what I was looking for. The dream was an Impressionist version of one scenario that could play out, depending on the choices many people, including you and Nate, make over the next few years."

"And you're here to help us make the right choices?"

"You have free will. Who am I to say what the right choices are for you?"

"Seriously? Since when have you not interfered with my life? Once you showed back up, I mean?"

"Okay, fine." She put on a fake hurt look. "I give you my opinion. But you make your own choices. Sometimes you'd be better off if you'd listen to me, but there you go."

"Colleen," I said. "Focus. The dream..."

"The unintended—but completely foreseeable—consequences of folks exploiting Stella Maris for profit would be a dangerous population level for an island only accessible by boat."

"Don't misunderstand," I said. "You know how I feel about resorts, condos, and all that. But we should be able to evacuate safely, right? The people who live here now, and with reasonable growth for a town this size? Blake has plans for all that. And modern forecasting is pretty accurate. We typically have at least a couple days' notice—plenty of time for everyone to get to safety."

"Those computer models aren't always that accurate. The U.S. model for Hurricane Sandy was off. All the models make educated guesses on some things. They aren't infallible. They give people a false sense of safety. And living on an island you have to take a ferry to seems idyllic until you have to get a lot of folks off in a hurry. And then there's the real nightmare scenario."

"There's one worse than in my dream?"

"Seismographs weren't around when the earthquake hit Charleston in 1886. But some folks figure it was more than a 7.0. I have it on good authority it was a 7.5. And it caused a slide in the ocean floor in Florida that triggered a small tsunami."

"An earthquake?"

"Charleston is in the bullseye for a major earthquake in the next fifty years. A slide along the Continental Shelf a hundred miles offshore could trigger a major tsunami with little warning."

"You're scaring me. Are you saying this is going to happen? This is not about men and free will. This is a God thing."

"You think God sends earthquakes and tsunamis?"

"No...I mean...Well, of course not."

Colleen sighed. "God set the world in motion. He doesn't use nature to punish us. That's Old Testament thinking. This is a New Testament world."

"No, I didn't mean that."

"Look, I never said there would be a hurricane, an earthquake, or a tsunami. But all of those things will happen at some point. It could be hundreds or thousands of years from now. The last time a major tsunami hit the Charleston area was eighteen thousand years ago. All you can do is keep your hurricane kit ready, watch the forecasts, and make sure building codes are what they ought to be. And don't let the island get overpopulated."

# TWELVE

I got home early, feeling pent up. Colleen's talk of all manner of natural disasters had left me unsettled, to say the least. I took Rhett for a short run on the beach. Sun-shot waves splashed playfully on the sand. Shore birds rose and dove in formation, calling out to me. The heady scent of the Atlantic worked its magic on me and my tension eased. I slowed to a walk, breathed in and out in rhythm with my steps. What was I supposed to do about a catastrophe that may or may not happen within my lifetime? A person could drive herself crazy worrying about such things.

A bubble bath. That's what I needed. "Come on, boy."

Rhett had more beach romping in mind.

"Want a cookie bone?"

Turns out he did. He scampered happily beside me back to the house.

I gave him his treat, then went upstairs and prepared my stress-relief bath—the one where I threw in lavender oil, a fizz ball, and half a dozen other things and turned on the jets. An hour later, I towel dried and wrapped in my fluffy green robe. Nate would be home soon. I could hear Mamma in my head admonishing me not to let my appearance go just because I had a ring on my finger.

I grinned, slipped into my favorite jeans and an off-the-shoulder summer sweater that was nearly the same blue as my eyes. I dried my hair, moisturized, and put on some mascara and lip gloss. My current favorite sandals, cream colored with a row of daisies on top, a simple chain at my neck, and a pair of silver hoops completed my carefully constructed I-just-threw-something-on look.

Nate pulled into the drive just as I finished dressing. I looked out the bedroom window and admired my husband as he walked towards the steps. If a man alive looked finer in jeans and a white button-down with rolled-up sleeves, I've never run across him. And mine had Chinese takeout.

I headed downstairs as he opened the front door.

"Slugger?" he called up the stairs.

"On my way down."

When I turned the corner and took the last half-flight down, he was waiting, smiling up at me. That smile never failed to set my heart to racing and wake a warm glow inside.

"Hey, how was your day?" I returned the smile.

"Productive. How about yours?"

"Productive and...stressful."

"We can't have that. What say we open a bottle of wine? Want to eat on the deck?"

"Let's." I went to gather utensils, napkins, glasses, and a bottle of La Crema from the kitchen.

I met Nate on the deck, where he had unpacked the food on the teak outdoor table. He opened the wine, and we fixed plates. We traded banter and devoured spring rolls, sesame chicken, and beef fried rice.

"Don't forget your fortune cookie, now," he said when we'd finished eating.

We each grabbed one.

I unwrapped mine and broke it open. *Be on the lookout for coming events. They cast their shadows beforehand.* Hell's bells. Colleen was into my fortune cookies now. I wadded up the slip of paper.

"What did it say?" asked Nate.

"It said be wary of handsome blue-eyed men. They have dishonorable intent."

"Why, that's entirely wrong. And I have the wedding band to prove it. Mine said, 'You will soon dance with your true love in the moonlight.' Now see? That's what a fortune cookie is supposed to be, right there. We need a refund on yours."

I stood and started to clear the table. "We have a lot of work to do. I've got several names we can erase from that ridiculous case board."

Nate looked at me with a tilt to his head. "Is everything all right?"

"I just didn't get enough sleep last night is all."

"Let's get done what we need to and get you into bed." His voice was husky.

"Why does that sound like you don't have sleeping on your mind?"

"I'm afraid I can't help myself. You're beautiful, Mrs. Andrews."

I smiled. "And you are a constant source of temptation, Mr. Andrews."

"Now that's good to hear." He grinned wide.

We finished straightening up, took our wineglasses into the living room, and settled into the sofa. I brought him up to speed on Paul Baker.

"Interesting," he said. "It's quite the quandary, because

we don't want to step all over an active investigation he's conducting based on an unsubstantiated suspicion. But if he's in hiding because of something related to our case, then that's another matter entirely, and we need to confront him."

"Agreed. But my instincts say he's laying low because he's nervous. He sent his wife and kids out of town to protect them—he wouldn't've taken the kids out of school this close to the end of the year for a vacation, especially not one he isn't participating in. And if it was something else—a death or illness in his wife's family—she would've simply told them that at work."

"You're right. It smells wrong."

"We need to ponder what to do about him." I sipped my wine. "Let's get to the case board. Shall I go first, or do you want to?"

"You go ahead," said Nate.

I approached the board, set my wineglass on one of the tables we'd spread the file boxes out on, took out my iPhone, and snapped a photo. If we needed to revisit anyone, we could. I picked up the eraser. "First, neither Williams nor Tallulah Poinsett killed their daughter. It's a travesty having their names up here." I erased them and told Nate about my conversation with Tallulah.

"And honestly," I said, "I feel silly having the entire congregation of a church on here. Yes, it's true, Shelby would've let any one of them in. But Tallulah said there was nothing controversial going on, Clint's crack about women in groups notwithstanding. I say we get rid of that silliness."

"As you wish."

I erased Members of St. Michael's Church. "And I told you what Tallulah said about the college friends." I erased

Lark Littleton, other college friends, and anyone unaccounted for in the address book.

"Now, to the book club ladies." I filled him in on all I'd learned while I was at the meeting, the note someone had slipped me, and what Colleen had picked up on after. "You know what? I'm just tickled pink that I can simply tell you what Colleen said, without having to make up some way I know what was going on in people's heads."

"I can see how that would be a relief," said Nate. "The Angela McConnell incident sounds promising. And we need to take a much closer look at Delta Tisdale."

Something twisted in my stomach. I was afraid of where Angela McConnell might lead us. "Agreed. But I want to erase everyone we can before we start talking about what's left. I'll feel less overwhelmed that way. We can focus. Though I am going to add Angela McConnell and erase 'nine other members' of the book club. If it was book club related, it was Angela or possibly Delta. I would've said Mary Bernard as well, but she has an alibi. And Colleen said not a single person objected to Nerissa Long joining next month, so the only book club drama was related to Angela."

"Sounds right. Erase away."

I made the Angela change. I erased Jane Kinloch, then Erin, Anne, and Liz, who were at a dinner party at Erin's house. Then Mary Bernard and Mariel Camp, who were at a dinner party at the Bernard home.

"Did you verify with Mary Bernard that everyone who was supposed to be there was present?" asked Nate.

"I did. Though she wasn't in a very good mood this afternoon." Mary Bernard impressed me as a woman accustomed to having her way. The book club business likely caused her to take to her bed.

"Are you finished with your erasures?" asked Nate.

I erased Evelyn Izard from under the book club heading. We'd actually had her on the list twice.

"Yes, and that felt so good."

"Well, you're about to feel even better. I've eliminated the folks at the two remaining charities, Charleston Library Society and Charleston Animal Society. That didn't take long. There's just not a whiff of a motive. And I have alibis for Cliff and Lisa Gerhardt, Bill and Brenda Gerhardt, Thomas and Deirdre Poinsett, Fraser and Constance Rutledge, and all Clint's army buddies."

I stared at him. "I thought I had a busy day."

"As much as I love impressing you, it wasn't as awe-inspiring as it sounds. Most of them were a short phone call, followed by two other short phone calls to verify. I spent odd moments between everything else on the phone."

"Nevertheless, your efficiency is remarkable. I declare, if you weren't my partner, I'd hire you and pay you good money." I took my eraser to the case board.

"Good to know. Maybe we could work out a bonus structure." His suggestive tone left no doubt what he had in mind.

"You're incorrigible. Tell me about the 'everything else' part of your day."

"I spoke to Sonya, and she says her husband was in jail on December 28 for violating an order of protection."

"Okay, so it wasn't Sonya's angry husband. But it could've been someone else's."

"I honestly don't think so. I've talked with everyone there is to talk to at One80Place. I've snooped around. There is simply nothing that leads me to believe anyone there was involved with this. I say we cut bait on that avenue of investigation. I'd erase that line as well."

"Happily." I erased Angry Shelter Husband and Board, Staff, Volunteers, Clients at One80Place.

"Now, let's see what we have left." I picked up my wine glass and joined Nate on the sofa. We surveyed our remaining possibilities:

| Suspect | Motives |
| --- | --- |
| Unknown Lover | Crime of Passion/Keep a secret |
| Charles Kinloch | |
| Sonny Ravenel | |
| Unknown Wannabe Lover | Jealousy |
| Spouse of Lover/Wannabe | Jealousy |
| Girlfriend of Sonny's | |
| Girlfriend of Unsub | |
| Book Club Member | Jealousy/Anger |
| Delta Tisdale | |
| Angela McConnell | |
| Evelyn or Edward Izard (Neighbors) | |
| Nick or Margaret Venning (Neighbors) | |
| Resident of Tent City | |

I said, "I need to add the new possible motive we have courtesy of whoever left the note in my purse. Well, maybe not. If it was Delta it was jealousy or anger, either over Clint or the book club."

"True enough. But Delta's not the only woman in Charleston who might've coveted Shelby's husband."

"Damnation. I'll add Unsub Pining for Clint later."

"But," Nate said, "our most plausible scenarios are, it was related to an affair Shelby had, this book club melodrama, or an unbalanced Delta and her 'crush' on Clint."

"For now I'll work the Angela McConnell angle and the other book club business, which crosses over to the Delta angle with Clint. Do you mind taking over Charles Kinloch and monitoring Paul Baker until we decide how to handle him?"

"Sounds like a plan. Then we can divvy up anything left standing."

"If I have enough time tomorrow, I'll take one set of the neighbors. We haven't spoken to either of them yet."

"Did you talk to Sonny today?"

"No," I said, "but not for lack of trying. I'm scared to death of where this Angela business is going to lead us."

"No sense worrying about it. If she knew Shelby was having an affair, that doesn't mean it was with Sonny."

"I know," I said, "but until we have another viable candidate for 'lover,' I'm going to worry. Sonny's my friend."

"He's my friend too. Let's not borrow trouble."

I sighed. "He's also our best resource to find out if Shelby ventured into Tent City, I think. I doubt Shelby would've told Clint she did that. He was very protective. And he was very forthcoming. I think he would've mentioned it if she went there and he knew about it."

"You're probably right."

"Wait. I know what to do about Paul Baker. What if we ask Fraser to call and tell him that he has to come pick up his last check? I seriously doubt Fraser's gonna pay that final bill, but I'm sure Baker's hoping he will. He could ask him to come to the conference room, where we could be waiting.

That way, if he is working a case, we don't blow his cover. And we have leverage. If Baker doesn't have satisfactory answers to our questions about the Shelby Poinsett case, we explain to Fraser how we verify trips to London. Which we'll likely do anyway, but Baker doesn't know that."

"Have I told you how sexy you are when you're brilliant? Come outside and dance with me in the moonlight."

And I did just that.

# THIRTEEN

I took Tallulah Poinsett at her word. She'd said helping would do her good, so I asked her to call Delta and ask that she come visit with her this morning for a spell. This was a request I knew Delta would simply never refuse as long as she drew breath. Her DNA would never permit it. If she had other plans, she would cancel them.

I street parked half a block from Rutledge on Queen and watched for Delta to leave. Sure enough, at nine forty-five, her Volvo passed in front of the intersection. I wouldn't be here as long today, so I left my car where it was and walked down Queen and around the corner to the front entrance of Delta's home.

Francina answered the door.

"Good morning, Francina, is Delta home?" I offered her my sunniest smile.

"No. You just missed her. I expect she'll be gone a couple hours. Can I give her a message for you?"

"It's the darnedest thing," I said. "I've lost my watch—the one my grandmother gave me? The last place I recall having it on was here yesterday. I hate to be a bother, but could I come in and look for it?"

"Why, of course you can." She stepped back and opened the door wider. "I'll help you look. What kind of watch is it?"

I stepped inside quickly. "Thank you so much. It's white gold with tiny diamonds around the face. On the back it's engraved, 'Happy Birthday Liz.'"

"I'll look in the living room and dining room," she said. "Why don't you look in the kitchen?"

Was she avoiding the kitchen after Colleen's spectacle in there the day before? "I'll do that, thank you again."

"Oh, no problem."

I walked down the hall and into the kitchen. After a moment, I called to Francina, "I don't see it in here. I'm just going to check the guest room."

"Oh, all right."

I slipped back into the foyer and bounded up the stairs. I had no clue which bedroom was the master. When I reached the second floor, I was in a sitting area. I knew which room was the guest room—I'd taken Francina's food there the day before.

Quietly, I opened the second door I came to. Definitely a teenage boy's decor. I closed it and moved on to the next. Also done in early teenager. Door number four led to a master suite, which might've once been a separate apartment. It looked to have been recently remodeled with a decidedly feminine flair—all yellow and cream. I moved quickly across the room to what I suspected was the bathroom door. Bingo.

I swung open the door to the medicine cabinet. Hell fire. She had a pharmacy in here. In addition to numerous over-the-counter drugs, there at least ten prescription bottles. I had no time to analyze the labels. I turned them all face-out and took pictures. Then I turned a few of the labels back around so they looked random as they had before.

I stepped back to the bedroom door and listened. Nothing. I put my head out into the hall and called downstairs, "Any luck, Francina?"

"Not yet."

"Me neither, I declare. I'll be down in just a second. I want to look one more place."

"Take your time," she called.

I moved to the closet. Delta had an extensive wardrobe and more shoes than Off Broadway. But it was the memory, photo, and hat boxes I was interested in. Or would she keep what I was looking for closer to her? I stepped back to the bedside table that held the things she'd use regularly— reading glasses, an alarm clock. Carefully, I slid open the top drawer.

Clint Gerhardt stared back at me from three photos scattered on top of a stack of greeting cards. They were all candid photos, taken at different events. In every shot he was talking to someone who wasn't in the picture, apparently unaware of the camera. I bet Delta looked at these every night.

This cast Delta's motives in offering up Sonny as Shelby's possible lover in a whole nother light. Could be she wanted that to get back to Clint—for Clint to believe Shelby was having an affair. Maybe Delta thought this would help him get over losing the wife he'd adored. Maybe she wanted to help with that in other ways. Was she that manipulative? I didn't touch the pictures, but snapped a quick photo.

I slid the drawer closed and dashed to the top of the stairs, pulling the watch out of my jacket pocket.

"I found it," I called.

Francina came out of the dining room. "Oh, I'm so glad.

That must mean a lot to you. Is your grandmother still with us?"

"No." A familiar sadness settled on me. "I'm afraid she's not."

"Can I see it?"

I held out the watch, still in my hand. Gram really had given it to me for my birthday.

"That is pretty. Mind, you get the clasp checked, now."

"I will. Thank you again. Are you feeling better today?" I slipped the watch inside a pocket in my purse.

"Oh, I'm fine. I always got on well with Miss Shelby. If she's hanging around here, that's fine with me. But everybody here might not be so happy to see her."

My head jerked up.

She gave me a knowing look.

"Francina, did you leave me a note in my purse yesterday?"

"What would I do that for?"

"Maybe there was something you thought I should know, but you couldn't risk telling me."

"Well, if I was smart enough to do that, I surely wouldn't be running my mouth about it now, would I?" She met my gaze and held it.

"No, I don't suppose you would." I slipped her my card. "If you ever need me for any reason, don't hesitate to call."

"That's good of you. You never know."

My cell phone quacked like a duck. A client. "Excuse me, Francina. Have a great day." I was out the front door.

"You too, now."

On the front porch, I glanced at the screen. Fraser Rutledge.

I answered the call on the fifth ring. "Liz Talbot."

"*Miz* Talbot. What have you got for me?"

"We're working a number of angles."

"Is that a fact? Well, don't keep me in suspense."

"We need to tie down a few things. How about we come by Monday morning at nine and bring you up to speed?"

"Very well. I will see you then."

"While I have you, I need a favor."

"What can I do for you?"

I explained our plan to get Paul Baker into his conference room, but didn't get into critiquing his investigative methods.

"I can make that happen," he said. "But I assure you that I will not be paying his final invoice."

"It never crossed my mind that you would."

"I am gratified to learn that we understand one another. You have yourself a real nice day, Miz Talbot."

Why in the hell had he not called Nate instead?

# FOURTEEN

According to the profile I'd pulled together early that morning, Angela McConnell had majored in communications at Hollins University in Virginia. She'd been an assistant something or other at WCSC Live 5 News, the local CBS affiliate, before landing the gig to become Mrs. Lamar Bernard full time. She'd quit her job right after the engagement announcement had run in the *Post and Courier*.

Currently, she was in the throes of wedding planning, something I knew a great deal about since Nate and I had just been through this in December. When speaking with Mary Bernard the day before about her dinner party, I'd chatted her up about wedding preparations—a subject she was delighted to hold forth on. This was how I came to know that Angela would be meeting with Mary and the wedding planner this morning at the Bernards' lower King Street home.

I drove by once to confirm Angela's BMW was in the drive, then circled back and pulled to the curb a block away. I grabbed a bottle of water from the cooler in the backseat. I might be here a while, and I needed to stay hydrated. The meeting had started at ten, but, at least in my experience, more often than not these things went long. Very long.

Just before noon, Angela rounded the corner on the sidewalk, heading back towards Broad on foot. Sonavabitch. I grabbed a map I kept handy for such purposes, opened it with a flick, and hid behind it.

Where was she headed? I was already pissed at this woman for what I was afraid she was going to tell me. And now I was going to have to chase her down to make her do it.

I waited, watched her in my rearview. When she was far enough away, I got out of the car, closed the door quietly, and took off after her. Staying just close enough to keep her in sight, I followed her up King to Market, where she turned right. Less than half a block later, she passed under the green awning and into City Lights Coffee.

Well fine, I could use a mocha latte. I followed her in, acting like I was preoccupied with important matters unrelated to her. The ambiance at City Lights was cozy and eclectic. The painted stamped tin ceiling, dark beadboard walls, and original art gave you the urge to sit a spell, if you weren't tailing a probable blackmailer.

Angela ordered her coffee for there, so I followed suit. I waited for my mocha, picked it up, and strolled over to her table.

"Well, hey!" I said. "Angela, right?"

She smiled real friendly. "Yes. Hey—you were at book club yesterday, right?"

I watched as she recalled why I was at book club and reckoned on all the things that could be about to go wrong. It was all over her face. I hoped this woman never played poker. She would lose all her almost-husband's money.

"That's right." I sat across from her.

She tucked a lock of her chin-length dark hair behind an ear. "It's good to see you."

"I'm so happy we ran into each other. I have a few things

I need to run by you."

"Well, I don't have but a minute. Just a quick cup of coffee. So much to do with the wedding coming up."

"Well, I guess if you don't have time, I could just talk to Mary."

Her brown eyes got large. "Oh, no. Don't bother her. What do you need?"

"What I need to know is what you were talking about with Shelby Poinsett in her library—the same library where she was later killed, I might add—after the December book club meeting."

"How do you—"

I kept my voice friendly, so as not to upset the other customers. "It doesn't matter in the slightest how I know. What I know is that you upset her...told her 'No one had to know,' that 'it was in her hands.' Now. I want to know *what* no one needed to know, and how *you* knew it. The price for your silence, that I already know. You wanted in that book club come hell or high water. Right?"

"You must be mistaken." She stood, as if to leave.

"Now you see, this right here is what they call poetic justice," I said.

She stared at me.

I smiled sweetly. "No one has to know. It's in your hands. Unless, of course, you killed Shelby, in which case, I promise you, many more people are going to know."

Angela sat back down. "You must be out of your mind. Of course I didn't kill Shelby. I was out with Lamar that night, with two other couples. We had dinner at Charleston Grill and a nightcap at The Belmont. In addition to our friends, any number of waitstaff can verify my whereabouts."

"I'll need the names of those friends. You can text them to me or write them down. Phone numbers too. And you can bet your mamma's pearls I'll be talking to everyone who was working at Charleston Grill and The Belmont. If there's a back door you could've snuck out of, I'll find it."

"You wouldn't embarrass me..."

"Angela, embarrassment is the very least of your troubles. Because from what I know right now, what you were doing sounds like blackmail, pure and simple. Start talking. And maybe, if you tell me everything I want to know, I'll forget to report that particular crime. Provided you can convince me it's the only one you've committed."

She ran a hand over her face. Looked around, like maybe she was planning an escape. Finally, she sighed, licked her lips, and fixed her gaze at a spot somewhere across the room. "I was having lunch with a friend back in early December at the Pavilion Bar."

Damnation. The Pavilion Bar was the rooftop bar at Market Pavilion, the hotel Shelby had frequented while Clint had been tracking her with the Find my Friends app.

"They put up Plexiglas and have heaters during the winter—you can eat up there anytime. Anyway, after lunch, we were riding the elevator down, and when we came out in the lobby, Shelby walked off the other elevator right in front of us. She was with a man—not Clint. They weren't on the rooftop. They had to have been on one of the guest room floors."

I made myself ask the question. "What did this man look like?"

"He was a black man—African-American."

I hadn't realized I'd stopped breathing until I started

again. Not Sonny. "Tall, short..." I made a rolling motion with my hands. Roughly a third of Charleston County was African American. I needed more to go on than that.

"He was tall. Very nice-looking. Late thirties, early forties I'd say. I had pictures..."

"You took pictures of them? Shelby didn't see you?"

"Yes, and no. There was a group moving from the elevators into the lobby. It's narrow there in front of the check-in desk. I walked fast, got in front of them, pretended like I was taking pictures of the lobby bar and Grill 225. It's very beautiful. Shelby was engrossed in conversation with him."

"What do you mean you *had* pictures?" I asked.

"After Shelby was killed, I got nervous. I was afraid of how it might look. I deleted them all."

I closed my eyes.

"You don't think he killed her, do you?" Angela asked.

I blinked, looked at her. "I have no idea. So, you threatened to tell Clint that Shelby was having an affair if she didn't let you in the book club?"

She had the grace to look ashamed. "Yes. I don't know what got into me. I've never done anything like that before in my life."

"How on God's green earth can being in a book club be that important to you? Couldn't you just start your own?"

"When I first signed up five years ago, it was all about being in a book club with that kind of history. And they're a service organization. They read mostly Southern literature and classics—some more recent novels, but good literature. I knew I'd have to wait, might not ever get in, and that was fine."

"What changed?" I asked, feeling sure I knew.

"Lamar's mother. Lamar is her only child. She idolizes him. And she wants to remake me in her own image. Book club is so important to her. And Lamar is the most important thing to me, so of course I want to please her." She teared up. "She just kept pushing and pushing it with Shelby. It got out of hand. All this wedding pressure. Everything piled up. I lost my mind a little bit."

"Yeah, I think maybe you did," I said. "Now I need those names."

# FIFTEEN

Walking back to my car, I tried Sonny again. Miracle of miracles, he answered the phone.

"We need to talk," I said.

"I have nothing more to say about Shelby Poinsett. To be honest, I'm a little pissed off that you think I was fooling around with a married woman."

"I don't think that."

"Coulda fooled me."

"Lookit, Sonny. I was doing my job, just like you do yours every day. I needed to ask you a question. You answered it. I apologize if, in doing my job, I have hurt your tender feelings."

He blew out a breath. "You made your point. What's up?"

"Meet me for lunch at the Pavilion Bar?"

He hesitated. "Why there?"

"Because it has gorgeous views of downtown and it's a lovely day."

"Right."

"I'm headed there now."

"I'm tied up until two."

"I'll wait. I've got some work to do."

*   *   *

The Market Pavilion Hotel sat on the corner of East Bay and South Market. I'd stayed there a time or two for special occasions. The accommodations were exquisite—Italian marble bathrooms, mahogany poster beds, and soft-toned bedding and drapes with sumptuous touches. I passed through the brass-framed revolving door.

The dark-paneled lobby bar was to my left, and the restaurant, Grill 225, to my right. A wide, elegant corridor with a few wingbacks, a couple tables, and an occasional chair served as the hotel lobby. I made my way through, then past the registration desk to the brass elevators. The concierge desk was situated just in front of the pair of elevators for guest use.

I took the elevator to the rooftop and scouted a table next to the railing overlooking Market. The umbrellas were up, providing shade. For once, instead of taking the chair with my back to the rail, I chose the one with the view of the Arthur Ravenel, Jr. Bridge, or, as I would forever call any bridge over the Cooper River, the Cooper River Bridge. Arthur's was the third one I'd crossed in my lifetime. It was a modern engineering marvel—an eight-lane, cable-stayed bridge, with two diamond-shaped towers completed in 2005—that had already become an iconic part of Charleston's skyline.

A waitress stopped by and I asked for unsweet tea for now, but told her someone was meeting me for lunch. I had work to do, and didn't want her to think my intentions were to tie up her table all afternoon drinking tea. Management would not be amused.

I pulled out my laptop and updated my notes. This case so far had moved so rapidly I hadn't had the time to do the extensive profiling of everyone involved that I ordinarily would, and that made me edgy. I had procedures that had served me well.

After I'd completed all the case notes forms, a clone of the FBI's FD 302, I started digging into Delta Jewel Reeves Tisdale. According to real property records, I'd nailed the value of her house, which had been deeded to her alone for one dollar last year, which I assumed was when her divorce from George Thomas Tisdale was final. There was no mortgage.

A subscription database gave me access to her basic information. She had no criminal record, but if there were domestic disturbances, they may not have ended in charges. Newspaper archives and another subscription database provided her educational background—she'd attended Agnes Scott College in Decatur, Georgia and graduated with a degree in Classical Civilization. What did one do with such a degree? No doubt there were opportunities I was ignorant of, or the college wouldn't offer the program. In any case, it had taken her five and a half years to earn her bachelor's degree. Had her education been interrupted by medical issues?

I pulled up the photo of the prescription drugs and commenced Googling. In addition to a few allergy medications and an antibiotic, Delta had in her arsenal: Lithium, a mood stabilizer; Abilify, a drug used to treat schizophrenia and bipolar disorders; Prozac, Paxil, and Cymbalta, all antidepressants; and Valium, most commonly prescribed as an anti-anxiety drug. Sweet reason, she couldn't be taking all of these at once, could she? The same doctor had prescribed them all. Perhaps he'd tried different drugs, moving from one to another to find what worked best.

Clearly, Delta had problems. But she'd seemed perfectly fine the day before. Perhaps the doctor had found a drug, or a combination of drugs, that controlled her symptoms.

I called Jane, who answered on the second ring.

We said our hellos and all that.

I said, "I know you and Shelby were best friends."

"Right."

"Who is Delta's?"

"Hmm...you know, I don't really think she has a best friend. I mean, she's friends with all of us, but she's really focused on her boys. And book club means a lot to her. I think she's a member of several other service organizations, but I can't recall which ones."

"How well do you know her?"

She paused. "Pretty well—I've known her most of my life. Why do you ask?"

"Does she have problems?"

"I guess we all do, don't we?"

I huffed an exasperated breath. Here was another one of those ladies who disliked gossip. "Good grief, Jane. You know what I mean. You must."

"How is this related to Shelby?" she asked.

"Well, now, I can't say until I know what *this* is. Have you ever known Delta to have violent mood swings, lash out at people?"

Jane was quiet for a long moment. "She's been doing real well lately."

"How long has she been doing 'real well?'"

"For the past six months or so. She had a bad spot during

the divorce. But the doctors have her on medications that seem to be working. You have to understand, when Delta is herself, she's one of the sweetest people you'd ever meet. Well, you met her. Would you have ever known she had issues?"

"No. But the fact that she does might be relevant."

"I just can't see how," said Jane.

I didn't mention Delta's crush or whatever it was on Clint. If Jane knew, I wanted her to tell me. "If she was really angry at Shelby, maybe about book club, maybe about something else...and she was off her meds—"

"No, just...no. I don't want to hear this. I don't want any part of it."

I glanced around me, kept my voice down. "But what if that's what happened? Don't you want the truth to come out? Or would you rather see an innocent man go to jail or death row?"

"This is preposterous. There must be another explanation."

"Can you think of any issue Delta had with Shelby aside from the book club controversy which they disagreed on?"

"No," she said. "And I refuse to believe Delta would've killed Shelby over such a small thing."

"But she could've if there were a bigger thing?"

"Excuse me, please. I have to go. I'm very sorry I can't help you." She hung up.

Hell's bells. I mulled Delta and her possible motives. The more reasonable of the two was her possible obsession with Clint. But if she was off her meds, reason wouldn't necessarily enter into it.

It was almost two o'clock. The waitress came by. I was

sorely tempted to order a pomegranate martini. I could've used one just then. I sighed and asked for more tea, a glass of sweet for Sonny, and some food menus.

I made a few calls and verified Angela's alibi. In addition to her friends, I called a friend in the food and beverage crowd who promised to call friends at Charleston Grill and The Belmont to see just how tight that alibi was. But truthfully, it made no sense for Angela to kill Shelby. Shelby was her only hope of getting what she wanted.

I glanced over my shoulder, past the pool. Right on time, the elevator opened, and Sonny Ravenel scanned the rooftop before walking my way. If Sonny and I hadn't practically grown up as brother and sister owing to him being my older brother's best friend, I might've gone out with him. He was a good-looking man, tall, lean, and toned, with broad shoulders and just enough of a bad boy vibe to attract the eye of most of the women between fifteen and eighty at the Pavilion. Sonny had never actually been a bad boy. He was one of Charleston PD's best detectives.

He slid into a chair at the wrought iron table. His dark brown hair was neatly cut, his hazel eyes wary. He eyed my laptop. "I hope you're researching better leads than 'Shelby was having an affair.'"

"Hey to you too, Sonny."

He grinned. "Hey, Liz. How's married life treating you?"

"Just fine, thank you. I ordered you a sweet tea," I said just as the waitress set it down.

He nodded at her. "Thanks."

She moved to the next table. I put my laptop away.

"I'm having the burger, no foie gras." I handed him a food menu.

He looked it over. "Eighteen dollars for a burger."

"We're paying for the view."

Sonny looked around, took in the view.

"Don't act like you've never been here before. You tell me you and Shelby were just friends? Fine. I believe you. But explain to me exactly why her husband never heard your name come out of her mouth, but her best friend and her mother know that y'all were tight."

"Fine," Sonny said. "Shelby knew Clint had insecurity issues. He got anxious about her spending time with friends who happen to be men. Shelby being Shelby, she didn't want to worry him. At the same time, she couldn't live her life like a teenager on restriction. End of story."

I reckoned on that for a moment. It fit. "Okay. Now tell me the rest of the story."

The waitress came back and took our order.

Sonny met my gaze and held it. "I don't know what you mean."

"According to her best friend, Shelby would never have had an affair with anyone inside their circle. You spent a lot of time with her, and you're not a part of that group. So, who else was she keeping company with?"

"How would I know? We were friends. I wasn't her social secretary."

"Was there anyone else at One80Place who she was especially close to?"

He thought for a minute. "No."

That confirmed what Nate had already gleaned. "Do you think it's possible she was trying to help some of the folks at Tent City?"

Sonny sighed. "She wanted to visit, talk to people, try to

get them to come inside. I had to persuade her some folks just aren't going to come inside a shelter with rules. Those who want to come inside will. Other organizations are working on how to help the rest. Shelby going out there to try to convince people just wasn't a good idea."

"And you're sure she never went?"

"Reasonably certain. I think she would've told me, even knowing I disapproved," said Sonny.

"When you and she had lunch, did you come here?"

"Sometimes. We had lunch at a number of other restaurants."

"Who did she talk about?"

"Mostly people we were working with—clients. Some of them had legal problems, some of them needed protective orders, things like that. She'd ask my advice."

"Who else did she talk about?"

"Clint mostly. Occasionally her parents. Jane. Fraser Rutledge. That's about it."

"So you don't have a clue of anyone she might have been seeing, really?"

"I told you. I don't think Shelby was having an affair. Shelby was in love with her husband."

I sighed, sat back in my chair. I didn't want to push him any further until after we'd eaten. We moved on to small talk, catching up on family. "Who's the girl you brought to The Pirates' Den a few weeks ago?"

"Nobody."

"You seeing anyone else?"

"As a matter of fact, I'm having dinner tomorrow night with someone you know."

"Really? Who?"

"Moon Unit Glendawn."

My jaw dropped. That's what was up with Moon Unit. She'd given up pining after Blake altogether. Did he know that? "You're not serious."

"Why wouldn't I be?"

I couldn't think of a reason. Moon Unit was smart, beautiful, successful. "I don't know, it's just—"

"You thought one day Blake would settle down with her."

"Maybe," I said.

"When's the last time you spoke to Blake?"

"I had breakfast with him yesterday, why?"

Sonny clamped his lips shut, made a face that said, *Too bad. I know something you don't know.*

"What?" I leaned across the table towards him. "Sonny. I mean it, you'd better spill."

Sonny's face took on a mulish look.

"You cannot seriously mean to leave me hanging like that." Who was Blake seeing? How could Sonny know more about my own family than I did?

The waitress delivered our food.

"Talk to your brother. Until then, it's in the vault." Sonny picked up his cheeseburger.

I was starving, so I followed suit. I would handle Blake later. I'm not sure any burger is worth eighteen dollars, but that one surely was good. When we'd finished eating, I leaned in a bit and asked, "Do you know of any black men Shelby was friends with?"

People that didn't know him well might not've caught the look that flashed across his face, then quickly disappeared.

He shrugged. "Lots of them, actually."

"Who?"

"Folks she volunteered with, some of the clients..." He gave his best imitation of an innocent face.

"Anyone in particular?"

He sighed. "Look. You and me? We've been friends for a long time. I don't like keeping things from you. But this, what you're chasing right now, it has nothing to do with Shelby's death. Can you please trust me on that?"

"I could if you would tell me exactly what you're talking about, and how you know for sure there's no connection to Shelby's death."

"I can't do that without violating another friend's confidence," he said.

"Shelby is dead. I don't think she'd mind."

"I never said it was Shelby's confidence. Gotta go." He stood, put money on the table, and left.

*Sonavabitch.*

I paid my part of the check and walked over to the bar. It was after three, and business had slowed a bit. I took a stool and ordered a Grey Goose pomegranate martini. I sipped it, sat back in my chair. A few minutes later, the bartender came over. "Are you in town for the weekend?"

"No, I live nearby. I don't get up here often enough. It's lovely."

"Can't beat the view," he said.

"No, you can't. Hey, listen, could you help me out with something?"

"Certainly. What do you need?"

I pulled out my phone and brought up a photo of Shelby. "Have you ever seen her up here?"

"Shelby Poinsett? Sure. She was a regular. I was real sorry to hear what happened to her. Nice lady."

"That's what everyone says. I never had the pleasure. I'm a private investigator." I showed him my license. "I'm working on helping to sort out what happened to her."

"I thought they arrested her husband."

"They did." I nodded. "But the case still has some unresolved issues. Did you ever see anyone else here with Shelby?"

"Yeah, as a matter of fact, the guy you had lunch with came in here with her sometimes."

I nodded. "Anyone else?"

"The guy she was most often with was an African-American gentleman. I don't know his name. He always paid with cash."

"Do you recall the last time you saw them in here together?"

"Probably the week before she died—Christmas week."

"Were they quarreling? Did they ever quarrel?"

"Not that I could tell."

"Were they demonstrative towards each other?"

"You mean holding hands, kissing?"

"Yeah."

He curled his lips in, shook his head. "Not that I ever noticed."

"Is there anyone else you ever saw her up here with?"

"Just her husband."

# SIXTEEN

I found a parking space with a view along Murray Boulevard and cued up a soothing playlist, one with lots of Kenny Chesney singing about St. John. Nate and I had spent our honeymoon in a St. John villa overlooking Cinnamon Bay.

I'd left most of my martini in the glass. Not that it wasn't delicious. But I was still working and would need to drive home after my next stop, the Izards. I'd told Nate I'd take one set of the neighbors in part because I wanted to spend some quality time with Evelyn. A notorious gossip was exactly what I needed just then.

She'd asked me to come at five, so I had time to call Blake.

"What's up?" he answered on the third ring.

"Franklin Blake Talbot. Who are you dating?"

"Mom?"

"Smartass. I take it this is someone you've seen more than once, or it wouldn't be such an all-fired secret."

He sighed a long-suffering sigh. "Who told you?"

"No one, and that's the point."

"Don't be dense. It's not flattering. Who told you I was seeing someone?"

"No one. I figured it out when I found out Moon Unit is

going out with Sonny tomorrow night." I took the high road and didn't throw Sonny under the bus, even though he was being difficult. Blake would assume Moon Unit told me.

"How are those two things connected, exactly?"

"Now who's being dense? You can't possibly be the only person in town who doesn't know Moon Unit's had a crush on you since we were in first grade. If that's the case, we need a new police chief. Too much gets by you."

He sighed again. "I've been seeing Heather Wilder for a couple of months."

"Heather...Wilder...from my case back in December?" That particular Heather Wilder had been the kept woman of one of Charleston's most eligible bachelors.

"Yeah. Hey, I owe you for that. What can I say? We hit it off."

I'd ended up with extra unplanned guests at Mamma's house for Christmas, my rehearsal dinner, and my wedding. Heather was smart—a grad student in environmental studies at College of Charleston. And she was gorgeous.

"You've been dating her since my wedding? That's five months, not a couple. Two. Two's a couple. Is this serious?"

"It could be."

"Blake..."

"What?"

"Does Mamma know?"

"No." His voice got defensive. "And your reaction is the exact reason why I haven't told any of you. So she's not a virgin. Hell, neither am I. And you shacked up with Nate before y'all got married. And you were married to his brother before that." Now he was shouting.

"That was completely different."

"How?"

I had nothing.

He said, "The point is, none of us are perfect. We all have pasts. And I like her a lot." He hung up.

"So do I."

Mamma was going to have a record-breaking conniption fit.


I squeezed into a parking place on Tradd and approached the Izard front door. It was cocktail hour, which was good. Alcohol might loosen Evelyn's tongue even further.

Edward answered the door. "Hello. You must be Ms. Talbot." He was fifty, give or take, though he had a well-maintained air about him. Here was a man who got regular manicures. Khaki pants and a button-down were a much better look for him than running shorts.

"I am. And you must be Mr. Izard."

"Please, call me Edward."

"I'm Liz."

"Won't you come in?" He stepped back. "We're having cocktails and oysters in the courtyard."

Oysters? This was May. Oysters weren't in season. "Thank you."

"What can I get you to drink? I have a pitcher of vodka martinis."

"That sounds perfect, thank you."

I followed him down the hall and out a single french door into the courtyard.

Evelyn was seated at a wrought iron table. She rose unsteadily as we arrived. How much had she already had to drink? "Liz, it's good to see you again." Her voice didn't slur. Perhaps she'd just stepped wrong.

We finished saying our hellos and making polite noises. Edward handed me a martini, and we all sat.

Edward said, "So you're working on the Shelby Poinsett case? Sad, that."

"Very sad," echoed Evelyn. "You know, when I had my gallbladder out last September, Shelby brought me casseroles. She offered to run errands for me. It took me several weeks to recover. That surgeon, I can't remember...what was his name, Edward? Anyway, I don't think he was one of the better ones, if you know what I mean. If I had it to do over again—"

Mamma would've lamented my deplorable lack of manners. But I had to stop her, or we'd've been there all night talking about her gallbladder. "Yes, I'm so sorry, Edward, to answer your question. I'm trying to cover all the bases. I understand you all were home the night Shelby was killed?"

"That's right," Edward said. "We've told the police and some other detectives, neither of us saw anything. We were home all day. I went out for my run in the morning. Aside from that, I don't think either of us even went outside."

Evelyn had finished her martini. "Edward, I'd like another, please."

He gave her a questioning look, but got up and retrieved the pitcher from the drink cart and refilled her glass.

"Unfortunately," he said, "we can't help you. I wish we had seen or heard something helpful."

"What about before that night?" I asked. "I understand from the police report that you all heard the Gerhardts arguing on occasion?"

Evelyn's voice was definitely slurring now. "It's hard to tell who was talking or what they were saying over the wall, to tell you the truth. We heard them out here, isn't that right, Edward?"

"That's right. I believe there were many heated exchanges. It was hard to make out what the trouble was. Our courtyard walls are quite thick."

"Is it possible," I asked, "that the people you heard arguing were from another house? It seems several backyards are across your courtyard wall."

"I suppose anything's possible," Edward said. "But I don't believe so. We should eat these oysters before they get warm. These are Charleston Salts from St. Jude Farms. Are you familiar?" He slid the tray of cracked ice filled with oysters on the half shell towards me.

"Oh, no thank you." I loved oysters, but only if they were cooked.

"St. Jude's is farming triploid oysters. They're going to extend oyster season, you watch. They're just starting the process. I have a friend who got me these." Edward offered the tray to Evelyn.

She picked one up, speared the meat with a cocktail fork, squirted it with lemon juice, and delivered it to her mouth. After a moment, she said, "Well, now, seems to me, the folks back behind us have had some trouble. There's some history there."

It was hard to focus on what she was saying. The oyster she'd put in her mouth had slipped back out and was stuck on her chin.

"Evelyn—" Edward made a motion with his napkin.

"Edward, I know those people have had the police over there and everything else."

I ignored the oyster. "You mean the house that faces Bedons Alley?" I squinted at her. Surely that was too far away.

Edward stared at the oyster on his wife's face. He was beet red.

She took a long sip of vodka. "I don't know which one it is. Might face Tradd, but the backyard's over this a-way."

"So you can't say for sure who you heard arguing?"

"It was the Gerhardts," Edward said. "Evelyn, you were hardly in a position to remember."

She reached for another oyster.

I looked away, then back. I needed to finish this and get out of here. "I wanted to ask you, Evelyn, about book club. Do you recall anyone being angry with Shelby over the wait list?"

The second oyster slipped out of her mouth.

Edward ran a hand across his eyes, slid it down the side of his face, and rested his chin in his palm.

Evelyn drained her glass. "What I heard was that several people were very upset. I overheard Mary Bernard talking to Mariel saying that Delta was going to speak to Shelby about it. Mary was not happy, as you can imagine."

"When?" I couldn't care less that she had two slimy oysters stuck to her chin.

"What I heard was that night. But Mary could tell you for sure."

"That night? The night Shelby was killed?"

"That's what Mary said. But now, I can't say that she actually came."

Edward said, "Evelyn dear, perhaps you should freshen

up."

"I don't need to freshen up, Edward. If you need to, go on ahead. I'm a grown woman. I can decide when I need to go to the bathroom. Would you pour me another drink, please?"

I stood. "Thank you so much for your time. Y'all have a great evening. Edward, please don't get up—I'll see myself out."

I crossed the courtyard as quickly as was decent, then practically ran down the hall and out the front door. I dashed to the car and called Mary Bernard.

We exchanged pleasantries, and then I asked her, "Mary, are you aware of any plans Delta had to approach Shelby regarding the wait list for the book club?"

Mary was silent for a long time. I thought the call had dropped. Finally she said, "As a matter of fact, I am. I had hoped not to become embroiled in this tawdry melodrama. But the truth is, Delta did tell one of the other members that she was going to talk with Shelby. Delta, as you know, is not in favor of a more liberal membership policy. She planned to plead her case to Shelby."

"When?"

Mary made me wait for it. "Well, it was the night Shelby died."

# SEVENTEEN

I had to wait for the six-thirty ferry, so it was seven when I got home. Nate had grilled salmon and made rice pilaf and a salad to go along. He was quite the chef. We finished our wine on the sofa in the living room and brought each other up to date.

Nate went first. "Do you want the details?"

"Not unless they're important. I have enough details for both of us."

"Paul Baker didn't leave the campground all day. I was able to get into the Kinloch residence for a solid two hours. Nothing on Charles's computer or in his office incriminates him in any way."

"I think we can forget Charles Kinloch," I said. "And Sonny." I gave him the highlights.

"So," Nate said, "Delta is almost certainly bipolar and has a...I can't call it a crush anymore. Three pictures in your nightstand of someone else's husband crosses a line. She has an unhealthy fixation on Clint Gerhardt. And she reportedly planned to see Shelby on the evening of her death, though we don't know if she did or not, and Shelby didn't tell Clint she was expecting anyone."

"Right."

"And whether Sonny likes it or not, or believes it or not,

Shelby was almost certainly having an affair with someone other than Sonny."

"Right again."

"Evelyn Izard, while a lush who can't hold her oysters, is a reliable witness in that she remembered overhearing the bit about Delta going to see Shelby."

"Yes," I said, "and she also believes the neighbors who they heard arguing were from another house. She wasn't clear on which one—the backyard lines are cobbled together back there. But she mentioned the police being called. If a report was filed, we should be able to find out where the neighborhood domestic issues were."

"And if we can prove there were other neighbors with issues, and no one can say for certain who was arguing, that piece of so-called evidence against Clint is neutralized. I'll talk to the Vennings tomorrow, see what they have to say, and follow up with Sonny."

"I want to spend some time trying to locate our unknown Romeo, and I'll definitely talk to Delta."

"Do you think that's wise?" asked Nate. "We certainly have an alternate theory of the crime there. If you tip her off, she has time to put together a defense—or run—before the police can question her."

I scrunched up my face. "It all falls together very neatly. Even if she claims she wasn't there, it's still a good theory. And yet...I just don't see it."

"Slugger, you haven't seen her off her meds. She'd be a whole different person."

"I know that's true, but think about this. What if she's navigated her divorce, stayed on her meds, is taking care of her boys, and yes, she has a thing for Clint, but that's really not a crime. Maybe it's a harmless infatuation. If she's innocent, being accused—questioned by the police—it could cause her to have a real setback. I just don't want to burden her with more trouble if she's not our killer."

"She certainly has the means to flee," said Nate.

I pondered that. "What if I ask Francina to confiscate her passport?"

"You think she'd do that?"

"Why not? Unless Delta tries to leave, she'll never know. If she goes looking for her passport, asks Francina about it, then we have Francina pretend to help her look, but get a message to us."

"I suppose that's reasonable. But you have to promise to be careful with Delta. You don't know what might set her off."

"But if she's on her meds, and she must be, I'd think she'd respond like anyone else. She might be angry, but I don't see her going for my throat."

Nate said, "Neither of us are doctors. And just because she took all her pills yesterday, that's no guarantee she will tomorrow."

"Point taken. I'll be on the lookout for trouble and call 911 if I need to."

"Oh, and I forgot, in my recap of your recap...The other thing you learned today is that Blake is dating a former courtesan."

"Mistress. She was someone's mistress. In unusual circumstances, yes. But, as Blake so eloquently informed me this afternoon, we all have pasts."

"You know I'm just messing with you. I like how you come to your brother's defense so quick. That's you Talbots. It's all fine and good for one of you to complain about the other. But God help anyone else who does." He grinned.

"That's all families," I said, then instantly regretted it. Nate's family was the opposite of that.

I watched his face change.

"I'm so sorry, sweetheart," I said.

"You're my family. You and the rest of those lunatics I married into."

My heart hurt. Clearly, I was too tired to talk.

My phone sang out a few bars of "Carry on My Wayward Son" by Kansas.

Blake's ringtone. He'd want to chew on me some more. I answered with a resigned sigh. "Hey, big brother."

"Hey. You talked to Sonny?" Blake's voice was tense.

My breath caught in my throat. Was this a trick question? Had he figured out Sonny had tipped me off about Heather? I stalled. "Since when?"

"This evening. We're getting ready for our set at The Pirates' Den. He was walking from his car to the house this afternoon, and somebody drove by and shot at him."

I bolted upright. "Is he all right?"

"Yeah, yeah. He's fine. Scared him shitless. They fired five shots. Whoever it was, it wasn't an experienced drive-by shooter. They've got an APB out on the car."

"Does he have any idea who it could've been? Related to a case maybe?"

"He says it could've been any one of a hundred people. He's locked up quite a few, and they all have friends and family."

I knew right then in my gut this was related to Shelby Poinsett. How? I bit my lip, winced. "Thank God he's okay."

"My thoughts exactly. That coulda gone all kinds of

wrong." He was quiet for a moment. "Hey, Lizzie. Look, I'm sorry I yelled at you before. You're my sister, and I know you're trying to look after me. I shouldn't've hung up on you."

"Aww...I thought you were calling to yell at me some more. It's all right. You were right. Heather's great, really. I like her."

"I need your help," Blake said. "With Mom."

"You want me to help you neutralize Mamma Drama?"

"Yeah. Please. She's—"

"You've got it. When are you going to tell her?"

"I reckon now that word's out, I'd better get it over with. Sunday, I guess. The way gossip spreads on this island, she'll probably find out before then."

"I'll help you talk to her."

We said our goodbyes.

I told Nate about Sonny. "It's connected," I said.

"How do you figure?" Nate squinted.

"I can't figure it. Yet."

# EIGHTEEN

Saturday morning, we got in our run, then scarfed down yogurt parfaits. It took Nate fifteen minutes to shower and dress. When I had to dry my hair, my record shower-dress-and-primp time was an hour. I hit that while he checked our tool and supply inventory in the back of the Explorer. I kept essentials in the Escape, but the bulk of our toy chest was in Nate's car.

We took both vehicles into Charleston for flexibility. Nate would talk to the Vennings, then try to catch up with Sonny. I was headed back to Market Pavilion Hotel. It was likely they had security cameras, but beyond unlikely they were going to let me see footage of guests. No crime had been committed in the hotel, and I wasn't a police officer with a warrant. But I had a backup plan.

I settled into a plush wingback between the lobby bar and the registration desk, against the wall and out of view of the desk staff. I pulled out my laptop. So many tools have been developed for private investigators over the last ten years. The technology Nate and I own is mind boggling. But one of the best tools in our arsenal is free.

It never ceases to amaze me what people will post on Facebook.

I opened the site. It detected where I was and offered to

show me what other people were saying about Market Pavilion Hotel. Oh, please do. This would've worked equally well from home. All I had to do was search inside Facebook for the hotel's name. But I couldn't follow up from home.

I clicked on the gear icon. First, I saw the hotel's page, with reviews. Then came what my friends were saying—oh, look at that. Tomorrow night was not Sonny's first date with Moon Unit. She'd posted a photo of them here two weeks ago.

Next came public posts. Here is where people get stupid. So many people have no idea what privacy settings are, or how best to use them. And it made my job so much easier. Still, sometimes it took a while to find what I was looking for. Sometimes I didn't find it at all.

I scrolled through strangers' girls' night out parties, check-ins, a video of a proposal taken inside one of the guest rooms, parents visiting college students, photos of champagne buckets, the ornate fixtures in the bathrooms...and many, many candid shots taken all around the property.

The posts were from total strangers, but that didn't matter. I was looking at who was in the background, the people who had no idea they'd been photographed, much less posted to social media.

Rehearsal dinners, anniversaries, someone having a large birthday cocktail on video. Tons of photos of the view from the rooftop. And Nitrotinis, a trademarked—literally—martini chilled with nitrogen. There were lots of photos of those. Vacation photos that belonged to people all over the world.

I scrolled to the end, then started over. I'd been scrolling through other people's precious moments for more than three hours when I found what I was looking for. A crowded lobby. A photo of friends sitting at the lobby bar. And in the background, Shelby.

With Eli Radcliffe.

Holy shit.

I stared at it long and hard. There was a crowd, and they weren't looking at the camera. But it was them.

The picture had been taken in October. Angela had seen Shelby in the same lobby with a tall, handsome, black man in early December. I right-clicked and saved the photo, zoomed in on Shelby and Eli, and cropped it.

I finished scrolling and scanning to see if there were more, but no such luck.

One was enough.

I pondered my best play. I knew I'd get nowhere with the front desk, concierge, or management. Guest privacy would be a critical component of their customer service playbook. The rooftop bar wasn't open yet. I couldn't show the photo to the bartender until later.

I was overthinking this. Ditzy blonde or shy blonde? I'd go with shy. I packed away my laptop, pulled out a pair of fake cat-eye glasses, put my hair in a clip and pulled several stands loose. I hunched my shoulders forward a bit and approached the front desk. There was a possibility the desk clerk, like the bartender, would remember Shelby by name and know she'd been killed. But maybe she wouldn't.

I waited until no one else was standing at the desk and approached.

"Hello, may I help you?" The bright-faced young woman oozed hospitality.

I dipped my chin and smiled nervously at her from under my eyelashes. "Well, I hope you can."

"I'll do my best." She was so eager.

"My sister and her boyfriend come here a lot. It's just hard for them to get quiet time alone. What with her three kids, and his four...anyway. They've had a tough time. And I really wanted to do something nice for them. A surprise, for next time they come in."

"What did you have in mind?"

"Maybe a bottle of champagne and some strawberries..." I lowered my voice, as if to utter something slightly naughty, "...maybe dipped in chocolate."

"I'm sure we can arrange that," she said. "What's your sister's name?"

"Well, she's Shelby...I'm not sure if they register in her name or his. Maybe sometimes one, sometimes the other."

The clerk tapped on her computer. "Last name?"

I gambled. "Poinsett." Surely she wouldn't give her married name. The bartender upstairs had referred to her as Shelby Poinsett and I hadn't thought a thing about it. Because she was a Poinsett, and this was Charleston. Her people were Poinsetts. Clint Gerhardt was from off. I'd bet good money she still had credit cards in her maiden name. But the bartender had mentioned Shelby came there with her husband.

"Okay," said the desk clerk. "It looks like they were coming in on Tuesdays. But it doesn't look like they've been in for a while. Did you want me to try the other name?"

"Eli Radcliffe."

More tapping. "I'm afraid I don't see that name. I could take your order and flag your sister in the system. We won't charge your card until they come in."

"Thank you, I appreciate that so much." I dug in my purse, pretending to look for my wallet. "Oh no. I'm positively mortified. I left my wallet at home. How long will you be here today?"

"Until five."

"Would it be all right if I go get my wallet and come straight back?"

"Sure. I'm Jocelyn, but anyone can help you."

"Thank you so much." I pulled my arms in to my body, hunched just a little, like a very shy, socially awkward person might do, and hurried out.

# NINETEEN

Nate, Sonny, and I met for lunch at Closed for Business. I needed thinking food, and their CFB Poutine was the best thinking food I'd ever come across. The guys were in a booth when I arrived, waiting for me. Heaven only knew how Nate had talked Sonny into coming given that he was avoiding the subject of Shelby with me.

We ordered—me the Poutine with an egg on top, each of the guys a Pork Slap, an also delicious and sinful concoction of fried pork cutlet, beer-braised pulled pork, pickled green tomato, swiss cheese, and house sauce on a brioche bun.

As soon as the waitress moved away from the table, I leaned across towards Sonny, keeping my voice low. "What in this world happened last night?"

He drew in a breath and slowly let it out, shook his head. "Some fool shot at me while I was walking from the car to the house. Five shots. I dove for cover. They missed."

Nate said, "Any ideas who it was?"

Sonny shrugged. "I didn't see who was in the car. The windows were tinted dark. The passenger side window was down, but it looked like the driver was shooting. That rules out any of my gang-related cases, I think. They're more efficient with drive-by shootings. There'd be a driver and at least one shooter."

I said, "Well, thank God it wasn't a competent criminal."

"The sheriff's office found the car abandoned not a mile from my house," Sonny said. "Owner says it was stolen, but he didn't report it. Likely because there was an outstanding warrant for him on an assault charge. But our paths had never crossed. Car probably was stolen, for the express purpose of shooting me."

"So why aren't you taking a vacation out of town while they sort this out?" I asked.

"Now how would that look? Liz, for cryin' out loud. I can take care of myself."

"I don't like it." I still had it in my bones that this was related to Shelby.

Sonny changed the subject. We chatted for a few minutes, small talk.

It was hard, but I didn't tell them about Eli, mostly because I suspected Sonny knew but wasn't telling me for reasons I couldn't imagine. Were Sonny and Eli friends? It was certainly likely their paths had crossed. Eli was a defense attorney, Sonny a police detective. They'd both been born and raised in Charleston. It was hard to imagine they didn't know each other. So was it Eli's confidence Sonny was keeping?

I needed to ponder this more and talk it over with Nate before I broached the subject with Sonny again.

"How did it go with the Vennings?" I asked Nate.

"Nice folks. They wanted to help, couldn't much. They did say it was entirely possible it was someone else they'd heard arguing. The houses through there are so close together. They said that, if it comes to it, they'll testify that they heard arguing, but can't say for sure who it was."

Sonny said, "I'm all for anything that helps Clint. But if these folks are changing their story, I need to let Bissell and Jenkins know. They shouldn't be blindsided by this in court."

"I'm hoping we aren't going to make it to court," I said. "But you can't be telling them anything about what we're working on. The Vennings haven't changed their story at all. It's how Bissell and Jenkins took it. They wanted it to be Clint and Shelby fighting. That fit their narrative of the crime."

Sonny was quiet for a long moment. "They're good detectives. This is a difficult case."

Nate, no doubt sensing growing tension, dove between us. "The best thing we can do is all focus on figuring this thing out before jury selection starts. Best for everyone involved if the charges against Clint are dismissed and Bissell and Jenkins get a new arrest. They look good. Everyone's happy. Am I right?"

"Of course that's what we all want," I said.

"Agreed," said Sonny.

"See," said Nate. "We're all on the same side here. Just like always."

I said, "Sonny, can you check into domestic calls in the area? See if any of the other neighbors were having loud arguments that might be what the Vennings and the Izards heard?"

"Yeah, I did that already. There's a couple two doors down who've had a domestic disturbance call. They could be the source of the commotion. I'll text you the names and address." He didn't sound happy about it.

The waitress brought our food, and we all dug in. I'd have to run an extra twenty-five miles to work this off. French fries covered in beef gravy with little shreds of beef, cheese curds, minced onion, and an egg on top. I may have moaned a little.

But my food didn't distract me from noticing how something was off with Sonny. I was more convinced than ever that he was keeping something important from me. I just had no idea why.

# TWENTY

Francina wore a wary look when she opened the door. Perhaps she guessed there would be a confrontation of sorts sooner or later.

"Hey, Francina, is Delta home?" Of course I knew she was. I'd looked down the driveway and seen her car.

"Yeah. She's here." She stepped back and opened the door wider. "If you'll wait in the living room, I'll go get her." I passed her the note regarding Delta's passport, with instructions at the bottom to tear it up and flush it down the toilet when she'd read it.

"Thank you," I said. "Are you doing all right today?"

She started to open the note. I shook my head and mouthed, *Get her first.*

Francina nodded. "I'm doing good. How about you?"

"I'm fine, thanks." I proceeded to the living room and pondered my strategy a bit more.

After a few minutes, Delta came into the room. She was dressed casually, in white slacks and a navy print blouse worn untucked. "Hey, Liz. Is everything all right? I wasn't expecting you."

"I'm so sorry for barging in," I said. "I need to talk to you."

"Please sit down," she said.

I drew in a deep breath, let it out. Her problems were none of my business unless she was there. "Delta, I understand you went to see Shelby the night she died."

She paled. Her lips parted, but she remained silent.

"Please understand, the last thing I want to do is cause trouble for you. But I need you to tell me the truth. Were you there?"

She looked around, seemed disoriented. Finally, she said, "I was."

Hell fire and damnation.

"Why did you go there?" I asked.

"Several members of the book club asked me to speak to Shelby. They were upset about her changing things, or at least allowing that possibility. I wasn't going to do it. But then I thought maybe if I could just share with her how some of the group felt...So I called her that evening, and she said sure, come on over, we'd have a glass of wine. I don't drink, but there's no reason Shelby would recall that."

I waited for her to continue.

"I got there a few minutes after nine. I'd fed the boys, and they were watching a movie. I just stepped out for a few minutes. They weren't by themselves long." Her eyes had a pleading look. It was important that I understood she hadn't neglected her children.

"What did Shelby say? When you spoke with her?"

She shook her head. Her voice quivered. "I didn't get that chance."

"Why not?"

"When I arrived, I rang the bell and no one came to the door. I knew Shelby was there—I'd just spoken to her. Lights were on. I worried something was wrong. I had no idea how

198 **Susan M. Boyer**

terribly wrong things were." Her voice broke. "I tried the door, and it opened, so I went inside, calling out her name."

"Wait, the door was unlocked?" I asked.

"Yes. I couldn't find Shelby downstairs, so I went up to the library. There was a glass of wine on her desk. I walked around and looked at what she'd been working on. I saw she'd written my name on the calendar. When I turned around..." Delta was crying now, staring at her hands.

"What happened?"

"I saw the end of one of the drapes hanging over the rail. I thought that was odd, so I stepped over to the doors, and that's when I saw Shelby."

"Behind you?"

"No, she'd already been pushed out the doors. She was in the courtyard. All twisted, but real still." She cried harder. "It was an impulse. I tore the calendar page out. I was afraid. I ran down the steps, and then I thought, maybe she was still alive. I didn't know who'd pushed her, if they were still in the house. But I went down the hall and out through the kitchen to see about her. She didn't have a pulse. There was nothing I could do for her. But...I was afraid of how it might look. I wiped my prints off the door and everything else I could recall touching and I came home to my boys."

"Oh, Delta. Why didn't you call the police and just tell them what you told me? Or find Clint?"

"Well, at that point, I had no idea what had happened. I couldn't process it, really. I was just afraid of how it would look."

"Why?" I knew the answer, of course. But I wanted her to say it so I wouldn't have to admit going through her things.

She stood, went to a console table, and grabbed a

handful of Kleenex. "Because there was this controversy, with me on one side and her on the other. And because I was diagnosed with bipolar disorder when I was eighteen. I'm being treated, successfully. But there've been times when my medications weren't working right or maybe I stopped taking them because I felt fine and I didn't want to take them. I've learned I can't do that. But there are incidents others could raise, if they wanted to, when I've flown off the handle. Acted irrationally, horribly. I smashed my husband's windshield once. I attacked a roommate in college. I've been in inpatient programs three times. Somehow, my parents kept it mostly quiet. The worst of it was when I was away at school. But I'm in a good place now. My medications are working. I would've never hurt Shelby. I cared about her, so much."

"And Clint?"

She flushed. "What about Clint?"

"Do you care about him?"

"Why, of course I do. We're all friends."

"What I mean is, do you have deeper feelings for Clint?"

She gasped, raised a hand to her mouth. "Why would you ask that?"

Why would I ask that? "Because I sense a change in your voice when you say his name. You seem a bit wistful. I'm a detective. I'm trained to notice things like that."

She stared at me for a good long while. "My husband left me and the boys because I have problems. I'm not perfect. He needs his life to be less messy. He's a selfish son of a bitch. And Clint is the exact opposite of Tommy. If I daydream about having a man that caring in my life, who does it hurt?"

"No one," I said. "As long as that's as far as it went."

"Of course that's as far as it went. For many reasons, but

mostly, I'm not that kind of woman."

"No, I don't believe you are," I said.

"What are you going to do?" Desperation seized her voice.

"I'm going to finish investigating this case. I have several other avenues to explore that have nothing whatsoever to do with you. Hopefully, I'll get to the bottom of it soon. If I can leave you out of it, I will. I have no desire to cause you more pain."

She nodded. "I appreciate that. More than I can tell you. A scandal might cost me my boys, though Heaven knows their daddy doesn't want to be bothered. That's the only reason I was able to get custody to begin with. But if anything goes wrong, his parents will pressure him."

"You have to promise me you are going to stay on your medications. Go about your routine. Don't panic and do anything self-destructive."

"And don't leave town?" she said.

"Were you planning on taking a trip?"

"No, that's just always what they say on television."


I pondered Delta as I walked up Rutledge Avenue on my way back to the car. I turned left on Beaufain, and was half a block from where I'd parked remembering how Colleen had told me to trust my instincts. My gut said Delta had told me the Gospel truth. It insisted this had more to do with something going down at Market Pavilion Hotel. Something Sonny knew about but wouldn't share. I'd bet good money that was why someone was shooting at him.

That thought had no sooner formed than I heard

*pfft...pfft.*

Something whizzed by my right ear.

I was tackled from behind, hit the sidewalk hard.

*Pfft. Pfft. Pfft.*

A silencer.

I raised my head to see the car.

Someone pushed me back to the sidewalk.

"Would you stay down?" Colleen said.

A car behind us accelerated.

After a minute, Colleen rolled off and let me up.

"Are you okay?" she asked.

"Skinned up, but otherwise fine. Who the hell was that?"

"No idea. I just had a 911 alert that you were in danger. I got here just in time to tackle you."

"Did you get a look at the car?" I asked.

"Older Cadillac—a big one."

"SUV?"

"No, a sedan."

I called Nate, then Sonny. Within moments, two patrol cars arrived, followed shortly by Sonny. Nate had been on a ferry back to Stella Maris, so by the time he arrived, I was almost finished giving my statement.

The four of us propped against my car and watched as crime scene techs searched for bullets. A uniformed officer came over and told us the car had been found, apparently abandoned on Montagu—two blocks away.

He looked at Sonny. "Looks like the same MO as last night. We haven't been able to locate the owner of the car. Outstanding warrants. His mother stated that last she knew the car was broken down in the parking lot of a Piggly Wiggly in North Charleston. The Pig's closed. We're still attempting to ascertain the location she referenced."

Sonny nodded. "Thanks. Keep me in the loop."

The officer went back to his vehicle.

Nate pushed off the car, moved over in front of Sonny. His voice was low and tight. "When those bullets match the ones they pulled out of your house last night, are you going to tell us what's going on?"

"Dammit to hell, Nate. You think if I had any idea who did this I wouldn't tell you? That's bullshit."

I said, "It can't be a coincidence."

Sonny ran a hand through his hair. "Of course it's not a coincidence. I just have no damned idea where the connection is."

"It's Shelby Poinsett," I said. "It has to be. That's all we're working on."

Sonny said, "See, that's the problem. I'm *not* working on Shelby's case. I never have. I have nothing whatsoever to do with it."

"What are you not telling me?" I asked. "What's the thing you can't tell me without violating a confidence?"

Sonny shook his head. "It's not that. And if I told you, you would agree with me. I'm confident of that. The thing I can't tell you did not get Shelby killed."

I sighed, shook my head.

Sonny said, "Maybe it'd be good for y'all to spend some time in Greenville."

"We have a case to work, thanks." I frosted my voice. "And I can take care of myself."

"With a little help from your friends," said Colleen.

# TWENTY-ONE

Sunday dinner at Mamma's house was always at two. That gave her time to finish frying things after church. We got there at one so I could help. I convinced Nate it would be best not to mention the shooting incident. No need to upset Mamma when there was nothing she could do.

We walked through the front door calling out our hellos.

"I'm in the kitchen," called Mamma.

We were meandering in her direction when a noise that sounded like a vibrating foghorn assaulted us.

"What the hell is that?" yelled Nate.

The noise stopped. From the backyard came Chumley's—Daddy's Bassett Hound—howl.

We quickened our pace towards the kitchen. Mamma presided over four large cast iron pans, two with chicken, one with gravy, and one she was just dropping okra into. I smelled biscuits baking.

"Mamma, what was that—"

The noise was louder this time. It drowned out Chumley.

Mamma rolled her eyes, her whole head, Heavenward. When the noise stopped she said, "You recall the didgeridoo on your father's Christmas list a few years back?"

"Oh no," I said. "I thought that was a joke—a scavenger hunt." Thank God I hadn't been the one to buy it.

"I'm sure it was just some of his nonsense at the time." Mamma pointed towards the backyard with her head. "He read something on the internet about how playing the didgeridoo is good for your breathing. He worries about his lungs, because you know how he used to smoke, way back. So now he's actually taken up playing that infernal thing. Elizabeth, see if you can distract him."

Blake walked into the kitchen. "Where is that—"

The noise recommenced.

"Liz," Mamma shouted over the racket.

"Okay, okay." I shook my head and walked out the screened porch door. I covered my ears and crossed to the center of the backyard where Daddy sat in a bar-height chair. The didgeridoo was five feet long and looked like a walking stick with a flare at the end.

The noise stopped. Chumley continued to howl, long and mournfully.

"Hey, Tutie," Daddy called. He laughed. We had an agreement he'd stop calling me that. I was pretty sure it was shorthand for Fruity Tutie, on account of my aversion to germs. Daddy had nicknames for everyone.

"Daddy, come inside and let's pick out a wine for dinner."

"I'll be in directly. I'm building up my time. Playing this thing's good for your lungs. How about that? They've got YouTube videos on the internet that teach you how to play."

Some days it would be a blessing if Stella Maris lost internet service.

"It's almost lunch time." I walked over and petted Chumley, tried to soothe him.

"Well, call me when it's on the table. Listen. I can make

the vowel sounds. You use your tongue—"

"Daddy, no. The neighbors are trying to enjoy a peaceful Sunday afternoon. It's too loud. We're going to have to find you a better place to practice if you're going to play that thing."

"A better place? Where would that be?"

"Someplace soundproof."

"There's no place like that around here."

"Maybe Blake knows of someplace."

"Nah. Nobody cares if I blow the horn for a few minutes in the afternoon. I'm not keeping anybody awake." He lifted the instrument to his mouth.

Blake would understand, I told myself. "Daddy, did you know Blake's dating one of the girls who used to live in that bordello down on Church Street?"

He lowered the horn, looked at Chumley. "Hound dog, hush up."

Chumley finished his howl, barked twice, then fell silent.

Daddy turned back to me. After a minute he grinned. "Does your Mamma know?"

"Not yet. But he's going to tell her today. Don't say anything yet." Aggravating Mamma was his absolute favorite thing to do in the world.

He stood and carried his didgeridoo towards the house. "Let's go see about that wine. Which one of the girls is it? They were all pretty."

"Heather Wilder."

Daddy grinned, nodded. "Pretty blonde."

"Now don't say anything to Mamma yet. Promise me."

"Oh, I won't."

He probably wouldn't. But he'd be waiting to bait

Mamma the minute Blake told them. We walked back into the kitchen. My sister, Merry, and Joe Eaddy, her boyfriend, had arrived. Mamma was giving Merry what for on account of she's the one who bought Daddy the didgeridoo.

"Well, if it helps his lungs, that's a good thing." Merry, the baby, could be depended on to take Daddy's side no matter what.

"You haven't heard what it sounds like," I said. "You got here too late for the recital."

"I can play it some more if you want me to," Daddy said.

"No." Mamma, Blake, Nate, and I all spoke at once.

"I'd like to hear it, FT," Joe said. FT was Joe's nickname for Daddy—Franklin Talbot.

"Joe," I said, "trust me on this. You would not. Daddy, how about a pinot noir today?"

"This won't take but a minute," Daddy said. "Joe, come on outside."

Mamma cut Joe a look. He wouldn't be asking about that didgeridoo ever again.

Blake looked at me, his face a confusion of apology, worry, and anger. "Sonny tells me someone took a few shots at you last night in Charleston. Why exactly did I have to get that news from him?"

Everyone froze, stared at me.

Daddy propped the didgeridoo in the corner. "What happened?"

I sighed. I couldn't really blame Blake. I'd thrown him under the same bus, he just didn't know it yet.

I shrugged, tried to look nonchalant. "I was walking back to my car over on Beaufain. Someone drove by and shot at me. Charleston PD is investigating."

"This something to do with a case you're working?" asked Blake.

"I don't see how," I said. "Possibly."

Blake and Daddy glowered up at Nate from under lowered brows. Their identical expressions said, *What are you going to do about this?*

Nate said, "Liz and I are going to be working as a team for a while instead of working different angles of the case."

"It may not have anything to do with me at all," I said. "It was a drive-by."

Blake said, "Just exactly like the one at Sonny's house Friday. What's the common denominator?"

I looked at him, shook my head. "We don't know of one."

Blake vibrated with tension. "You know that doesn't make sense, right?"

I nodded. "I do."

"You have some idea, sis." Blake stared at me.

I sighed. "I can't talk about a case, Blake. You know that."

Mamma, who had been unaccountably quiet, said, "Why don't y'all come stay with us for a few days? Until the police figure this out?"

"That'd be the best idea," said Daddy. "Safety in numbers."

"Daddy, we're fine," I said.

Nate said, "Frank, if I thought Liz was in any danger at home, we'd be right here. Or we'd go to Greenville for a few days. But the security we have at the house covers the entire property. No one is going to drive by and shoot at Liz there. This particular criminal seems to have a particular MO that doesn't translate well to the island. He's stealing cars from folks with outstanding warrants who don't report them stolen. Then he drives by—he's not a great shot—and he ditches the car right after. If he tried that here, we'd have him at the ferry dock."

Daddy and Blake seemed to mull that.

"It seems to me that Nate has this under control," Mamma said.

My mouth started moving before I could stop myself. "And it's a good thing, because Heaven knows, Liz is incapable of taking care of herself."

"*E-liz-a-beth Su-zanne Tal-bot.*" Mamma enunciated each syllable precisely. "You should thank the Good Lord that you have family who care about you."

"I'm very grateful for my family," I said. "I just wish they had a little more faith in my professional abilities."

"We do," Merry said. "But you have to admit, your job carries risks that none of the rest of us have to deal with. We worry because we love you."

Blake cleared his throat. As the police chief of Stella Maris, his job also carried risks. But the crime rate was low in our quiet, isolated town.

Merry hugged Blake. "We love you too, big brother. You just avoid trouble better than Liz."

I shot her a lethal look.

Nate said, "We've got this. Really. There's nothing to worry about. Carolyn, that fried chicken smells amazing."

Joe's eyes lit up. "Fried chicken. In all the excitement I missed the fried chicken. Oh man."

Joe's fondness for Mamma's fried chicken bordered on Pavlovian.

Mamma said, "Girls, set the table in the screened porch.

It's nice outside."

I moved to the sink to wash my hands. I scrubbed for two minutes with hot water and soap, then pulled the hand sanitizer out of my purse. When I looked up, they were all staring at me. "Would y'all prefer I didn't wash my hands before I handle your dishes and silverware? I've been loving on Chumley."

"Yeah, wash up good," said Blake.

With the focus off my close encounter with bullets, I had a passing fear Daddy might circle back to the didgeridoo. Looking to put more distance between us and that god-awful horn, I said, "Daddy, do you know what I saw this week?"

"What?" He gave me an inquiring look.

"A Vietnamese pot-bellied pig," I said. Daddy's fascination with animals of any sort was well-established.

"A pig? Where'd you see him?" Daddy asked.

"At someone's house. I was doing an interview. I had no idea how big they can get. For some reason, I thought they were smaller."

"Was she a pretty pig?" Daddy asked.

"Well...I guess that's a subjective thing. She was cute, I thought."

"A pig," Daddy murmured. He pressed his lips together, gave his head a little tilt. It was a thoughtful look. Then he said, "I'm going to open some wine. Joe, Nate, Blake, let's get out of the women's way." He headed towards the den.

Merry said, "I think one Sunday they should make dinner."

"Would you want to eat it?" Mamma asked.

"Nate's a great cook," I said.

"Your daddy can't make himself a sandwich," Mamma

said.

Merry and I found safe conversation territory in Daddy's pretend helplessness, which Mamma enabled. We carried flatware, napkins, condiments, et cetera, outside and set the table while Mamma finished cooking.

Mamma called us all to dinner and prayed over us, throwing in an extra petition for protection for all of us, especially me. We piled our plates high with fried chicken, biscuits and gravy, mashed potatoes, okra, macaroni and cheese, butter peas, broccoli casserole, cucumber salad, and cantaloupe, then settled into chairs at the long, rustic table in the screened porch.

Mamma said, "Did y'all hear Tammy Sue Lyerly has gotten her real estate license?"

Between bites, we all said, "No."

"She hasn't sold anything yet," Mamma said. "But she's got several listings."

"Real estate's been slow for the last year," said Blake.

"What's that?" said Daddy.

"There's several houses that've been on the market for more than a year," said Blake. "That's unusual. Property here usually moves fast."

"That'll drive property values down," said Joe. "Any idea what's going on?"

Blake made a face. "Nah, it's strange. I've heard stories where several agents had serious buyers back out last minute. A couple times I've heard them say they were concerned about evacuating in a storm."

A bolt of electricity stabbed me straight through the heart. Was Colleen popping into other folks' dreams with Impressionist nightmares? I looked at Blake.

"What?" He stopped, his fork halfway to his mouth. "What's wrong? I told you I have that covered."

"Do y'all ever worry about that?" I asked.

Daddy scowled at me. "Well, of course it's something we all think about. It's not just a Stella Maris problem. Evacuating Charleston County is the bigger issue. With forty-five new residents every day and a thriving tourist population, it's a huge problem. Add Berkeley and Dorchester County, and it's a logistical nightmare."

"I get that, of course," I said. "But we're at greater risk because for us there's no road out."

"That's why we have to be vigilant," said Daddy. "You were at Clemson when we evacuated before Floyd hit Cape Fear. But you have to remember the rest of us coming up there three days before the storm made landfall. Only reason we weren't sitting in that mess on I-26 for nine to ten hours with everybody else. Eighty percent of Charleston County evacuated. Still more tried to leave but gave up. State's made a lot of changes in procedures since then. I hope it's enough. You were eight when we left before Hugo hit. I know you remember that."

At the time I'd wanted to stay and watch the storm. A child's folly. I had no idea. "I remember." The destruction had certainly left an impression. Still, I'd been young. Perhaps I needed to reflect on the days and months after we'd returned more.

Daddy creased his face at me. "We can't sit around worrying about things that might happen. We have to be prepared and take action when we need to. What's wrong with you? You look like you've seen a ghost."

Because I had. "Nothing," I said. "I'm fine."

Everyone had finished eating, and we were sitting around the table chatting, when Merry said, "Joe and I have news."

That got everyone's attention.

Merry said, "We're getting married." She held up her left hand. A large diamond glittered on her ring finger. She must've slipped that off earlier, or I would've noticed it.

The table erupted in congratulations, hugs for them both, admiring the ring—happy noises.

Finally, Mamma said, "Have you set a date? I need to reserve the church. We don't want to have to do things last minute." She cast me a look. Our wedding had been much too hastily planned to suit her.

Merry got quiet. We all looked at her expectantly. She looked from one side to the other. "We've decided against a big wedding."

Mamma said, "Well, of course. Whatever you want. We can keep it small. Family, friends..."

"We were thinking smaller," Merry said.

Mamma looked confused, like Merry was speaking in tongues.

"Instead of having a huge wedding—which was so much fun when y'all got married." She looked at me. "But we just did that, right? We're thinking we'll just go on a dream vacation and get married."

"A destination wedding?" Mamma's face announced her displeasure. "I know those are popular, but...where did you have in mind?"

"Patagonia."

Mamma was speechless. This happened so rarely, we all sat there and watched to see what would happen next.

"It's a bucket-list trip," said Merry. "We'll spend three weeks in Argentina and Chile. We'll get to see the Andes, the glaciers—it's so beautiful there. And we're going to take the End of the World Train trip."

I was stunned. "That's not a destination wedding. You're eloping."

"Well..." she said. "It's not really eloping if we tell you we're going."

Mamma found her voice. "How can you not want family at your wedding?"

"It's not that, Mamma," said Merry. "It's just that we don't want all the fuss. We want this to be about us starting our life together, not how many people are going to be at a table."

Merry had an up-close view of wedding planning when Nate and I had gotten married. She'd said then if she ever got married, she was going to run off and do it. It never crossed my mind that she was serious.

Mamma sat back in her chair. She looked profoundly unhappy.

Daddy cleared his throat. He looked at Merry with something approaching disapproval, which was nearly as rare as Mamma being struck mute. "You'd better get your mind on something sensible."

Joe smiled, kept his eyes on Merry, waiting for her to handle us.

She was my baby sister. I sighed, did a mental eye roll. "I think if that's how they want to get married, that's exactly what they should do. Merry's only going to get married once."

Daddy lower his chin and raised his eyebrows at me. "We hope that's how it works out anyway."

"We don't expect you to pay for this." Merry's patience was running threadbare.

Daddy said, "It's got nothing to with money. People with any common sense at all don't run off to the farthest corner of the earth to get married where nobody can come to the wedding except a bunch of pygmies you've never met before."

"The pygmies are in Africa, Dad," said Blake.

Daddy turned to Blake. "Whatever they are down there, they've never met your sister. But they'll be in her wedding pictures instead of us."

I said, "Daddy, this is a trip of a lifetime. It's an adventure."

His face looked like he'd eaten bad shrimp. He looked at Mamma, shook his head. "Where does she get this stuff?"

Mamma looked close to tears. I kicked Blake under the table. We needed a distraction, fast.

Blake said, "Mom, when I get married, we'll have another big to-do. You can invite the whole town."

Every head turned to stare at my brother. This was a very un-Blake thing for him to say.

Innocently, Daddy said, "You got your eye on anyone in particular?"

Blake said, "As a matter of fact, I've been seeing someone I got to know at Liz and Nate's wedding."

Mamma's head came up. "You have? Who?"

"Heather Wilder," said Blake.

Daddy said, "Aww, she's a pretty girl." He regained some of his natural jocularity.

"She's the—" Mamma moistened her lips. "Was she one of the young ladies who spent Christmas with us? From the…house on Church Street?"

"Yeah, that's right," said Blake, like he had no clue this would be controversial.

"Now, Mamma," I said. "There's no difference in what she was doing and what a lot of girls do these days. The circumstances were unusual, but—"

"Does she like children?" Mamma asked. She'd no doubt been worried she may never have grandchildren at the rate we were going.

Blake grinned. "She loves them. But now, let's don't get in too big of a hurry here. We've only known each other a few months. All I'm saying is that *if* I ever get married, you can plan as big a party as you like. Liz's wedding was a lot of fun."

Daddy said, "Bring her around next Sunday, why don't you?"

Mamma looked at Merry. "This is what you really want?"

Merry reached for Joe's hand. He took it and stayed quiet. Joe was a smart man.

"It's what we really want," said Merry.

"Well," Mamma said, "then that's what you should do. A marriage is much more important than a wedding." She didn't quite smile. But we all knew she would make her peace with whatever made Merry happy.

And whatever made Blake happy.

# TWENTY-TWO

I steeled myself as Mercedes led us into Fraser Rutledge's office that Monday morning. This could get sticky.

"Miz Talbot, Mr. Andrews." Fraser stood and walked around to the front of his desk.

Eli rose. He'd been sitting in the same chair as the first time we'd come here.

"Would it be all right if we sat over here?" I pointed to the conversation area in the corner across from Fraser's desk. "It looks so much more comfortable."

I watched as Fraser's genetic code, which mandated hospitality and manners above all else, warred with his desire to have the power seat behind the desk. Eli watched as well. He would take his cue from Fraser.

Fraser extended an arm towards the sofa and chairs. "By all means. Let us be comfortable."

Nate and I took seats on the sofa, Fraser in a leather chair at a right angle, and Eli across from him in a matching chair.

"I hope you have good news for me," said Fraser.

"We have news," said Nate.

Fraser leaned in. "Well, let's hear it."

I took a deep breath. "Eli, now would be a good time for you to tell us all about your relationship with Shelby."

Eli's head, slightly tilted in an expression of attention, straightened. "I don't know what you mean."

Fraser's forehead creased. His eyes squinted.

I said, "We have photographs." Okay, we had one photograph, but one was enough.

"Eli, what the devil is she talking about?" Fraser's voice coiled, like a snake preparing to strike.

Eli stared at me. "Photographs? Of what?"

"Of you," I said. "At Market Pavilion Hotel. With Shelby. We know you were meeting her there every Tuesday."

Fraser's eyes grew hard and dangerous. "Talk to me, Eli. Now, dammit."

Eli turned his head to the left, rolled in his lips, shook his head. "It's not what they're making it look like."

Fraser said, "Well then, what exactly is it, pray tell? I thought you did not know Shelby, Eli."

Eli sat back, crossed his legs. "All right. All right...Fraser, you know I grew up poor. I killed myself working my way through college, law school."

Fraser nodded, his countenance dark. "I am aware."

"What you don't know about, what I don't talk about, is my sister. She didn't go to college. She, uhh...she's had a rough time. I've tried to help her. She'll do fine for a while, get a job. I'll help her get an apartment. But somehow things always go sideways for her. Her name is Ruth. My mother liked biblical names.

"Ruth has a two-year-old little boy. And she's expecting again. The, uhh...the father is a different man. A god-awful excuse of a man. He's been in and out of jail. He uses Ruth. Tries to get her to hit me up for more money."

Eli paused, stared at the floor.

We waited.

"She's my little sister, Fraser. And this good-for-nothing piece of trash made her drive him to the store one night last April. She had no idea he was going to rob the place. He killed a man for less than a hundred dollars. Now my little sister is going to jail. There's a plea bargain. But she's going to do time. And I have no idea how to take care of two little children. We don't have anyone else."

He cleared his throat. "Ruth is out on bail right now. I have a friend. A police detective."

Nate and I exchanged a glance.

Eli said, "By the Grace of God, this was his case. I got her a good lawyer, of course. But we have to make arrangements for the children. I cannot. Let. Them. Go. Into. Foster. Care. My friend, the detective. He introduced me to Shelby. Said maybe she could help. Shelby was...like you said, Fraser. An angel. But Shelby couldn't have children. We'd been meeting at Market Pavilion so that Shelby could get to know Ruth. It was a private place, that's all. Shelby'd get a suite. We brought in lunch. Shelby wanted to adopt Ruth's children. Ruth was real close to saying yes. Real close."

He looked at me. "I was the last person on the planet who would've hurt Shelby. She was the answer to my prayers. Now I'm going to have to figure out how to raise a two-year-old and a newborn. And it's not that I don't want them. I've just never had to take care of kids, and Simone..." He looked away. "My wife. She doesn't want to take the kids. We have a different kind of life. Two careers. It's not ideal, for sure. But we'll be okay." He nodded like he was trying to convince himself.

"Let's see these pictures you have," Eli said.

I pulled out the blown-up image of Eli and Shelby walking through the hotel lobby. Eli took it, looked at it, then pointed to the edge, to something I'd cropped out. "That's Ruth's head."

Fraser snatched the picture from Eli, stared at it. "Eli, why in God's name did you not tell me any of this? I could have helped."

"Because I'm an officer of the court, just like you. We have clients who care about our image. This firm...we've worked damn hard for where we are. I wanted to keep this mess quiet. I didn't want it to touch us. No one connects me with Ruth, and God help me, I wanted to keep it that way."

"Your friend, the police detective," I said. "Sonny Ravenel, right?"

He looked at me. "That's right. Sonny didn't—"

"No." I shook my head. "Sonny didn't say a word. Did he ever meet with you and Ruth and Shelby?"

"Yes," Eli said. "A couple of times. He's helped a lot with getting Ruth a decent deal. He knows the solicitor assigned to the case. He spoke up for her, said how she was helpful, told the truth right off."

I nodded. "Sonny's a good guy. I've known him most of my life. Did you know someone shot at him Friday night? A drive-by."

"I hadn't heard," said Eli. "Is he all right?"

"He's fine," said Nate. "So is Liz. Someone took a few shots at her Saturday evening. Same MO."

"Now that is interesting," said Fraser. "Thank the Good Lord you are both unharmed."

Nate said, "The only connection—the only thing they are both involved with—is Shelby's case and the people around it.

Is there any way, Eli, your sister's boyfriend is upset that y'all were planning to have his child adopted?"

Eli made a face. "I can't see it. He didn't want the child. Tried to force my sister into an abortion. Would his friends go after Sonny? Absolutely. But Shelby? No."

"You have sure as hell rattled somebody's cage," said Fraser. "And that's progress. The first progress we've had in a while. Good work."

"There's just one thing that troubles me," I said. "Surely Shelby would've discussed a subject as serious as adopting children with Clint. But he had no clue what she was doing at Market Pavilion."

Eli closed his eyes, sighed heavily. "Shelby said she wanted to wait until Ruth agreed, or was close to agreeing, before she mentioned it to Clint. Apparently they'd discussed adoption before, and he had some reservations. You see, this is why I didn't want this case. Fraser, I know you believe Clint is innocent. But all along, I've had it in my gut that Shelby finally spoke to Clint about adopting Ruth's children the night she died. My suspicion, my burden, is that they argued, and either accidentally or on purpose, he sent her out those french doors."

Fraser's eyes glittered. It was hard to tell what he was thinking. He glared at Eli. "Rest your worried mind, my friend. Like I told you, Clint did not kill Shelby. Not because she wanted to adopt your sister's children. Not for any reason."


Mercedes escorted us to the conference room. The massive Palladium windows looked out over Broad Street. Paul Baker sat at the conference table. He was dressed in a golf shirt and khakis. He looked up as we came in. An expression of distaste slid over his face.

"The hell is this?" Baker stood.

Mercedes made the introductions.

Nate said, "Relax, Mr. Baker. We just need a few moments of your time."

I smiled sweetly. "You must be real busy. We've tried and tried to get a hold of you. I'm so happy business is good. Mercedes, we'll holler if we need Fraser."

Mercedes nodded, backed out, and closed the door.

Baker sat back down.

Nate and I took seats across from him, facing out the windows.

"Now," I said, "perhaps you could explain to us how it is an experienced, highly regarded detective such as yourself could spend four months on a case, bill a trip to *London* to verify an alibi, and not come up with anything better than the victim must've been having an affair with one of Charleston's best police detectives?"

Baker's face slid into neutral. His tone went all casual like. "I got nothing against Sonny. But the evidence leads where the evidence leads."

Nate said, "Exactly what suggested to you that Sonny was having an affair with Mrs. Gerhardt?"

"The friend—Delta what's-her-name," said Baker.

I nodded. "We spoke to Delta as well. But she told us that you bullied her into giving a name."

Baker raised a shoulder. "I don't bully. She said what she said."

"And exactly what was that?" asked Nate.

Baker spread his hands, tilted his head. "She said Mrs. Gerhardt talked about Sonny a lot."

"And from that you extrapolated an affair?" I asked.

"Process of elimination," said Baker.

"Did you find any evidence that Sonny was having an affair with Mrs. Gerhardt?" Nate asked.

"I was pursuing several leads," said Baker, "when I was removed from the case."

"Do tell?" I said. "What might they be?"

Baker said, "Nun-uh. This is your case now. Find your own damn leads, if you're so damned smart."

"Here's what I think," I said. "I think you felt comfortable throwing Sonny under the bus because you knew that would never stick."

"Why the hell would I do that?" asked Baker.

"Because someone paid you not to investigate this case," I said.

He stilled. After a minute, Baker screwed up his face. "What the hell are you talking about?"

Nate said, "The only question remaining is, are you also performing drive-by shooting services for your client? Are you missing on purpose? Trying to scare Sonny and Liz?"

Baker said, "You're outta your freakin' minds. I don't shoot at people for anyone. And that's a hell of a thing for you to suggest."

"Well then," I said, "if it wasn't you, based on your knowledge of the case, who do you suppose it was? Because I assure you, Sonny and I both narrowly escaped being shot."

Baker stared at a spot on the wall above our heads.

I said, "Is there a reason, Mr. Baker, why your wife and children have left town two weeks before the end of the school year and you are living in an Airstream trailer less than ten miles from your house?"

He looked startled. "You've been following me?"

"Of course we have," said Nate.

I could see the wheels spinning in Baker's head. If we could find him, so could someone else. We were all quiet for a few moments, waiting each other out.

Finally, Nate said, "Here is how this is going to go. You're going to tell us who was paying you—aside from Fraser—to work, or not work, this case and why. You're going to tell us everything you know, and what you suspect. Because if you should fail to do that in the next five minutes, I'll call Mercedes, and she'll get Fraser in here. And we'll tell him how we verify alibis in London—how any competent investigator would. And then you can explain to him why you spent three nights in London in regards to a murder that happened right here in Charleston. Then we're going to call Sonny. And you can imagine how he's not feeling kindly towards you right now. And we're going to explain to him our theory about how maybe you fired shots at him Friday night."

Baker raised a lip, huffed out a breath. "If I'da shot him, I wouldn'ta missed."

"Then tell us who might have," I said. "Save your career."

Baker gave me a look that said *puh-leez.* "There's no way you're not telling Fraser everything we say."

I lifted a shoulder. "Maybe he won't press charges if you help us. You took his money to do a job, then took someone else's to *not* do a job. Fraser's a very good attorney. Want to see how many charges he can spin out of that?"

"You don't have a damn thing on me," Baker said.

Nate looked at him levelly. "Is that a fact? Are you willing to bet your freedom on that?"

We both stared him down.

Finally, Baker shook his head. "I never liked this to begin with. Fraser and Eli have given me a lot of business. I'm done. People are getting shot at. If he'd been able to find me, I'da been the first one to go. I'm a loose end. That's why I sent the wife and kids to her sister. Keep them safe."

"If who had been able to find you?" asked Nate.

"Right after I caught the case, I got a call. No idea who it was. God's truth. It was a burner phone. Sold at a convenience store in Summerville, but no camera. Guy says he wants me to make sure I don't look hard enough to find anything. Offers me a hundred grand. I got kids headed to college in a few years."

"And did he pay you?" I asked.

"Fifty grand up front. The other fifty after the trial," said Baker. "Only reason I haven't left town."

"How was the money delivered?" asked Nate.

"He told me to be on Meeting Street, near the Circular Church, at six p.m. and wait for a call. Called at six fifteen and told me to check behind the Hutson-Peronneau Vault in the graveyard. Money was there in a duffle."

"How much have you spent?" I asked.

"Not a cent," said Baker. "Not one damned cent."

The door opened. Fraser stood there, looking like the Wrath of God. The speakerphone on the console had been on the entire time. "I ought to have your ass locked up, and I just might do that yet."

Baker shook his head in disgust. "I shoulda known."

Fraser sauntered into the room, Eli behind him.

Fraser said, "Paul, I always liked your wife. She is a good

woman. You've got nice kids too." He leaned on the conference room table, palms flat. "See precisely how helpful you can be to Miz Talbot and Mr. Andrews here. Be damned sure you do not fail to answer the phone one solitary time should they call. *If* they figure this out in spite of your disgraceful breach of trust which nearly allowed an innocent man to be tried for murder—put at risk of his very life—*if* they are able to accomplish this *before* the trial and *if* in fact there is no trial for Clint Gerhardt, *then* I will consider allowing you to keep your freedom. Now get your sorry ass the hell out of my sight."

# TWENTY-THREE

That afternoon, we went back to the case board. Nate paced and alternately squeezed and tossed a stress ball in the air. I sat on the sofa. Rhett alternated sitting by me and following Nate. I made some adjustments to our case board and we pondered the remaining possibilities.

| Suspect | Motive |
| --- | --- |
| Unknown Lover | Crime of Passion/Keep a secret |
| Unknown Wannabe Lover | Jealousy |
| Spouse of Lover/Wannabe | Jealousy |
|      Girlfriend of Sonny's | |
|      Girlfriend of Unsub | |
| Book Club Member | Jealousy/Anger |
|      Delta Tisdale | |
| Evelyn or Edward Izard (Neighbors) | |
| Nick or Margaret Venning (Neighbors) | |
| Unknown Wannabe Lover (Clint) | |

"What about Ruth?" I said. "Her boyfriend may not have wanted her unborn child, but what if there was an emotional exchange between her and Shelby? Shelby would've let her in the house, no doubt. She likely would've welcomed a chance to spend more time with Ruth. Maybe Shelby thought she'd finally introduce her to Clint."

I moved to the desk and pulled up the photo of Eli and Shelby, the original, uncropped version. To Eli's right was a woman whose head reached his shoulder. "I'll start a profile on her."

"All due respect to your empathy for the woman, but my money is on Delta Tisdale," said Nate.

I shook my head. "I just don't believe that." I zoomed in and studied Ruth more closely. A lovely woman, she favored Eli.

And then I saw it. "Hell's. Bells."

"What?" said Nate.

"Come look at this."

He moved behind me.

"Look at this guy, two people back from Ruth, in the crowd. See those bright blue sunglasses with wings?"

"Yeah, but I can't make out who that is, can you?"

"Not clearly. And that's the point. He doesn't want to be recognized. But I've seen those sunglasses before. I have a strong suspicion that is Edward Izard. And the skinny redhead on his arm? Is most assuredly not his wife."

Nate leaned over my shoulder and squinted at the screen. "Pull up another photo of Edward Izard."

I Googled him and selected images. He appeared on the screen with Evelyn at a variety of events, and a few times with a young woman in her early twenties who was a younger version of Evelyn.

Nate said, "They just have the one daughter?"

"And one son." I suddenly wished I hadn't zoned out while Evelyn had been chattering on and on at book club. "When Colleen stayed at book club after I left, Mariel Camp was thinking about how Edward was having an affair with a girl his daughter's age."

"That could be him," Nate said. "But with the sunglasses, and in a crowd…it's not a clear enough image to say for sure."

I clicked back to the digital photo from the hotel lobby and studied it some more. "Oh, it's Edward all right. This explains everything."

I called Delta.

She answered on the second ring.

"Delta," I said, "I need to ask you something confidentially."

"Of course," she said. "Anything I can do to help." The eagerness in her voice didn't escape me.

"Tell me about the Izards. Clearly they're wealthy. Was that her family money, his, or both?"

"Well, Evelyn was a Middleton," she said, as if that explained everything.

"Okay, but that family tree has many branches, some leafier than others," I said.

"Evelyn's parents left her several hundred million dollars. She was an only child."

"And Edward?"

"Well, of course the Izards had money. But the story is that his father lost it all in one failed business venture after another. My understanding is that Evelyn and Edward have an ironclad prenup. If they divorce, he gets nothing. If anything happens to Evelyn, a sizable portion of it goes to charity. Evelyn didn't tell me that herself, you understand. But it's common knowledge."

# TWENTY-FOUR

Sonny agreed to meet us at The Pirates' Den for dinner. Stella Maris was safer for all of us. It was a Monday night, so the island's favorite restaurant/bar/hangout wasn't crowded. We grabbed a table by the window overlooking the ocean and ordered a pound of boiled shrimp and a pitcher of margaritas to start. The owner, and customary bartender, John Glendawn—Moon Unit's father—delivered the margaritas himself.

"Shrimp and grits is the special tonight," said John. "Y'all ready to order or you want to work on this a while?"

My mouth started watering. "Shrimp and grits for me."

Sonny and Nate both echoed my order, and John headed back to the kitchen.

"Sonny? I get that you felt you couldn't betray Eli's confidence," I said. "And I admire that. But now that he's told us the whole sad story about Ruth and how Shelby wanted to adopt her children, we can talk freely amongst ourselves, right?"

Sonny seemed to mull that for a minute, then said, "It looks that way."

I showed him the photo I'd printed out of the man I believed was Edward Izard. "Have you ever seen this man before?"

230 Susan M. Boyer

Sonny took the photo and the magnifying glass I handed him. "It's hard to say for sure it's the same guy from this photo. But one Tuesday right before Christmas, Shelby and I were coming down in the elevator. Eli stayed behind to spend some time with Ruth and his nephew. Most of the time Ruth stayed overnight in the room Shelby had already paid for. She was taking advantage of the luxury, knowing what lay ahead for her.

"Anyway, Shelby and I walked out of the elevator and this guy with a redhead—her I recognize—came off the other elevator. I guess they were involved with each other, not looking where they were going. They ran right into us. Literally. They started apologizing, then Shelby and the guy recognized each other. Both of them looked shocked. It was a little awkward. She introduced him as her neighbor. I don't recall the name. He introduced the redhead as his niece in from out of town. We all said hello. They apologized again for bumping into us. Shelby was afraid he would think there was something inappropriate going on between us. And that was that."

"Except it wasn't," I said.

"Explain," said Sonny.

A waitress set a platter of boiled shrimp on ice with slices of lemon on the table. We all reached for shrimp, but kept talking.

"Did Shelby mention anything else to you about the incident?" I asked.

Sonny shook his head. "I wouldn't call it an incident. Some guy and his niece bumped into us. They apologized. That was all."

"Sonny." I cocked my head to one side. "Did you buy that

was his niece?"

Sonny shrugged. "I never gave it any thought. Shelby didn't contradict it."

"I'd bet Gram's silver that was his mistress," I said.

Sonny mulled that a minute, chewed on a shrimp.

Nate said, "You and Shelby felt awkward, you said. You were thinking how it looked for y'all. But Edward Izard—that's Shelby's neighbor—he was worried about how it looked *to* y'all."

I explained the rumors about the Izard prenup. "We need to get ahold of a copy of that document."

Sonny's forehead creased. "You're thinking Edward killed Shelby because she saw him with another woman and might tell his wife?"

"Exactly," I said. "And now he's taking shots at you."

"But why wouldn't he have done that months ago?" asked Sonny.

"My theory is that he likely tried. He's not a very adept criminal. Shelby was easy. If my theory is right, he rings the bell, she sees her neighbor, maybe is a little nervous because she hasn't told Clint yet what she's been doing at Market Pavilion hotel. She lets him in. Either she invites him up to the library where she's already having wine, or she goes to get her glass and offers to bring him one. Either way, he follows her upstairs and pushes her out the window. She never saw it coming because it either never occurred to her that he was having an affair, or she just figured it was none of her business."

Nate said, "With you, it would've been much harder because you didn't have a relationship with him. Also, it would've taken a lot more nerve to directly attack you than

Shelby. He would've used an entirely different method. Do you remember anything unusual happening around that time?"

Sonny squinted. "Like what?"

Nate said, "Anyone following you. Maybe a break-in."

"He would've preferred it to look like an accident, I'm thinking," I said. "Especially coming right around the same time as Shelby's death."

Sonny was quiet for a long moment. "Two things, now that I think about it. Son of a bitch. I had a gas leak the night before Shelby died. Fortunately, I smelled the stuff they put in natural gas to make it stink when I opened the door. Never flipped the light switch. Called the fire department, later a plumber. I figured old house, old pipes. A potential disaster I was lucky to avoid.

"Two nights later, I was coming home from work and my brakes failed. Fluid leak. I thought it was just a run of bad luck. But if it was Edward, why would he stop there?"

I said, "My guess is when no one questioned him regarding Shelby's death, he figured you didn't remember the incident in the hotel, or you didn't think it was significant."

"Which was in fact the case," said Sonny.

"This feels right to me," I said. "Edward would've had the resources to bribe Paul Baker. After he was fired and we were hired, maybe Edward decided he needed to clean up his loose ends. Probably went looking for Baker, but couldn't find him. Edward escalates, takes a few shots at you. After I came to his home, he figured maybe I suspected him, so he decided I was a risk as well. The guy's a fanatical runner. My guess is, he stole cars from depressed neighborhoods, did quick drive-bys, ditched the cars, and ran home. Guy like him out jogging at night doesn't fit the profile of a shooter."

"We have a workable theory of the crime—crimes," said Nate. "Now all we have to do is prove it."

# TWENTY-FIVE

Nate dressed in running togs and followed Edward when he left the house at one that Tuesday afternoon. We had in earpieces to communicate.

I waited in the lobby of Market Pavilion Hotel wearing a grey wig, stage makeup, granny glasses, a frumpy dress, and sensible shoes.

At 1:05, Nate said, "He ran to the end of Tradd. Now he's barely jogging. I'm having to walk to stay far enough behind him."

At 1:10, Nate said, "He's slowed to a walk. Now he's headed in the door. Yeah. Runner my ass. He's just running around. Handing him off to you."

I looked up as Edward walked in the door. Surreptitiously, I took several photos as he checked in and walked towards the elevator. Then I stood and followed him.

"Oh, could you hold the elevator, please?" My voice was feeble.

"Yes, ma'am." He pressed a button, and the doors stayed open.

I stepped onto the elevator.

"What floor?" he asked.

"Oh, I'm going up to the rooftop to meet my granddaughter for lunch," I said.

"Lovely day for it," Edward said.

"It is, isn't it? She's such a sweetheart."

When he got off on the third floor, he said, "Have a nice lunch."

"Thank you so much, young man." I pressed the button to go back to the lobby. I glanced toward the front as I made a U-turn off the elevator and moved quickly towards the ladies' room. Nate sat at a table in the lobby bar by the window. "He got off on three," I said into my mic.

I passed through the elegant vestibule and into the bathroom. Inside a stall, I removed my wig and changed clothes. Then I moved to the mirror and used makeup remover wipes to clean the little old lady off my face.

"Here's the redhead," Nate said into my earpiece. "I'm headed to the elevator. She's picking up a key."

A few minutes later, I heard him say, "Ladies first," and then, "Three please." He'd let her on before him so she'd swipe her key, then asked for the floor he knew she'd press before she pressed it. At least that was the plan.

I listened as they rode in silence.

A few minutes later, Nate said, "I slipped the transmitter into her purse. She went into 326. It's at the end of the hall. Any number above 320 will work."

I rolled up my granny outfit, stuffed it into my purse, and went to check in. "Could I please have room 326? My husband and I stayed there the weekend we got engaged. It has sentimental value. He's meeting me this evening."

"I'm so sorry, ma'am." The fresh-faced, eager-to-help clerk today was a young man. "That room is taken."

I gave him my best distressed female look. "Oh no. Well, what's the next closest room available?"

"I could offer you 328 or 301. I'm afraid that's all we have on the third floor."

"Three twenty-eight, please."

I gave him my ID and credit card, and a few minutes later I had a key. I took the elevator to the third floor, and Nate and I went into room 328 and set up our receiving and recording station.

In case we ever needed it, we recorded what went on in room 326 that afternoon. Nate put on the headphones and listened so I didn't have to. We needed to know when they were leaving.

An hour later, Nate laid down the headphones and picked up the camera. We listened as the door to the next room closed. I quietly opened our door, and Nate stepped out into the hall long enough to snap a picture of the two of them cuddling and sucking face as they walked towards the elevators.

# TWENTY-SIX

Tallulah had another chance to help us find Shelby's killer. At my request, she called each member of the book club and asked them to meet at Delta's house for a special tribute to Shelby the following morning. It was such short notice, no doubt many would've been unable to come except for Tallulah's plea. We'd traded heavily on the bond between women over the last few days.

When everyone was assembled, Tallulah spoke eloquently, but with difficulty, about Shelby's life, the things that were important to her. Tallulah announced a new program for the homeless, named in Shelby's honor, and funded by what would've been her inheritance.

Then everyone grazed at the vast spread of pretty sandwiches, salads, canapés, dips, crudités, pastries, tarts, fruits, cheeses, and nuts that Francina had whipped up in a culinary coup unrivaled since the loaves and fishes miracle. I doubt my mamma could've pulled off such a feat.

While everyone socialized and ate, I mentioned in strictest confidence to several of the women, including Evelyn, that the police were returning to the Gerhardt residence the next morning to fingerprint the back gate, which they knew the killer had used to access the courtyard. Through some oversight, the gate had been missed during the initial forensics evidence collection.

Our theory was that Edward knew Clint was on the third floor listening to music. Perhaps he could even hear it on the other side of the wall. But not knowing when Clint would decide to come downstairs, Edward would've gotten out as of there lickety-split, then slipped into the courtyard thru the gate to make sure Shelby was dead. On the outside chance he'd gone thru the kitchen, he surely wouldn't've gone back inside. He would've left via the path behind the house and then gone out the gate.

At my request, Delta suggested to Evelyn that she should be sure to let the neighbors know so they wouldn't be alarmed should they see all the goings on. Of course, there was only one person we wanted to make sure Evelyn told.

My mission accomplished, I stood alone by the sideboard in the dining room and reached for a cucumber sandwich.

"Put a few of those in your purse for me, would you? And some ham biscuits." Colleen faded in, in ghost mode.

I glanced around to make sure no one was within earshot. "I will do no such thing. But I will get you some ham biscuits later at the Cracked Pot. Provided I get an answer or two from you first."

She gave me this serene, angelic version of a poker face. "What do you want to know?"

I switched to throwing my thoughts at her. *Are you running off home buyers? From the island? Giving them nightmares and all such as that?*

"What do you think?"

*Colleen.*

"I might occasionally tip folks off as to how it's not smart to get too many people on an island with no bridge. It's in their best interests."

*What about the people who already own those houses?*

"Eventually they'll sell them. But I need to keep housing values down. Then people will stop building new homes there. I told you. We have to keep the population down."

My thoughts went back to after Hugo. *What's coming? When?*

Colleen sighed. "Something. Sooner or later. I'm looking at things on a whole different timeline than you. We've got to find you a comfortable balance between panic and unconcerned."

*Thank you so much.* I might've been the teensiest bit cranky. *That's very helpful.*

"Stay calm. If anyone asks, tell them living there's a pain because you have to get on a ferry to go to work. And the mosquitoes are horrible." She faded out.

I looked at the cucumber sandwich in my hand. I'd lost my appetite.

# TWENTY-SEVEN

I waited inside the courtyard on one of the chaise lounges by the pool. I'd turned it so it faced the back of the house.

At 10:35, I heard the gate swing open.

I walked around the back of the house. "Edward, that you?"

Silence.

I turned the corner.

He was three feet in front of me.

"You couldn't be sure, could you?" I asked.

"Of what?" His voice was a scoff.

"That you hadn't left your prints on the gate. Of course the police fingerprinted it the night Shelby was found. There were no useable prints. A shame."

"I don't have the vaguest idea what you're yammering on about," he said.

Then he rushed me.

He wore gloves this time, and carried a knife. I saw the glint in the moonlight that peeked out from between the branches of the live oak.

I lunged to the side, darted backward into the courtyard.

"I can't understand why you'd kill Shelby," I said. "She probably didn't even realize you were having an affair. If she had, she wouldn't've told Evelyn. That wasn't her way. You didn't know your neighbor very well, did you?"

He lunged at me again with the knife. He wasn't feeling chatty yet.

I slid out of reach. "You couldn't take the chance, could you? If she'd have talked, Evelyn would've surely divorced you, and you would've been left with nothing. That would be hard for someone like you. You've never worked a day in your life, have you, Edward?"

"You don't know a damned thing about me or my life. Impudent bitch." He thrust at me.

Again, I parried.

"So why are you trying to kill me again?" I asked.

In answer, he charged at me.

I spun away, put a chaise lounge between us.

"You should've brought your gun," I said. "That would've been much easier. I'm younger and quicker than you are. If you were actually running as much as you pretended, it would be a whole nother story. This could take a while. But you had no idea I'd be here, did you? You probably brought the knife just in case, right? Did you bring it along the night you killed Shelby?"

He darted around the chair.

I danced away.

He crouched, spread his arms and legs.

"Had you planned to stab her?" I asked. "So much easier, I imagine, to shove her out the window. Much neater. No chance of getting blood on you. Of course, she would never in a million years have expected such a thing from you."

I circled him, stayed out of reach.

"Damnable women," he muttered.

"I know, right? First there's Evelyn. She drinks a lot

these days, bless her heart. Do you think that's because she knows you're having an affair?"

"Evelyn's been an alcoholic her entire life. She drank too much long before we married."

He lunged at me again.

I scooted out of reach.

He was breathing hard, disheveled. "And if you think I'm going to let you or that damned do-gooder Shelby Poinsett rob me of everything simply because I sought comfort in the arms of a sympathetic companion—refuge from the disgusting drunk my wife has become—you, my dear, are sadly mistaken."

I lunged towards him.

He stepped back, surprised.

"So you, what, rang the bell, asked Shelby if she had a moment to talk? I bet you feigned crying on her shoulder. She probably couldn't resist helping a neighbor."

"She had a soft heart. It was her undoing. Just as your overestimation of your own abilities will be yours." He lunged at me again.

I juked right.

"Did she see it coming? When you pushed her out the doors?"

"That was the best part. The look of shock on her face. I really didn't expect to enjoy it quite so much, the element of surprise. On the other hand, I'm going to enjoy killing you even more."

The courtyard flooded with light.

"Drop the knife and lay down. Hands behind your head."

Bissell's voice came from above, from the very french doors where Edward had pushed Shelby out. He and Jenkins had filmed everything.

Nate stepped from behind Belly's house, gun drawn. "Drop the knife and get the hell away from her."

Sonny came from the walkway behind the house. "On the ground. Now."

Edward looked from Sonny to Nate. He froze, but didn't drop the knife. I could see him seething. "I don't think I will." He let out a guttural cry, leaned forward, and charged me.

I dropped to the ground.

Sonny fired one shot.

Edward Izard fell in front of me.

# TWENTY-EIGHT

Before Mamma could read about what had happened in the paper, I called and gave her the high points. Blake knew we'd been working the Shelby Poinsett case, so I called him too. No use in anyone worrying unnecessarily. Nevertheless, come Sunday, Nate and I had to retell everything gathered in Mamma's kitchen with the whole family. And Heather Wilder, who'd been invited before we knew we'd have drama.

Mamma had to hug me close, then fuss at me long and vehemently about taking chances. She gave Nate what for too.

"Carolyn, I promise you, I was there the entire time. Sonny too. Plus two other veteran Charleston Police detectives. We had three guns trained on Izard. Liz was wearing body armor under her clothes."

Mamma had tears in her eyes. Her stony expression telegraphed *I trusted you with my girl.*

Nate blew out a breath, ran a hand through his hair. "That said, I aged two decades in the split second I waited for Sonny to take that shot. I would've taken Izard out the next instant. There's no way he was going to hurt Liz." Nate looked to Blake for support.

Blake stared at him, shook his head. "Mom, you know how hard-headed Liz is. There was never anything Nate could do to keep her from doing what she damned well pleased. And he had to let Sonny take Izard down if at all possible. Sonny has the badge."

"Language, Blake." Mamma turned her displeasure on him.

Heather cast Blake a sideways glance. "I hope you don't mean you think Nate *should* be able to control Liz. She's a grown woman."

I knew for a fact Merry and Blake were both happy I'd done something to distract Mamma from their love lives.

Blake swallowed hard. "Now that's not what I meant."

"Well, I hope not," said Heather. "Because Liz can take of herself just fine. I think it's exciting."

Slowly, Mamma turned to look at Heather. It wasn't The Look she gave her. But there was definitely a warning there.

Heather averted her gaze.

"How is the Izard man? He going to make it?" asked Blake.

"Yeah," Nate said. "He'll live to stand trial. Charges against Clint have already been dropped."

Merry shook her head. "It's just so awful. Shelby Poinsett was literally killed for being in the wrong place at the wrong time. And she was there doing such a loving thing. Those poor children."

"Eli Radcliffe is a stand-up guy," I said. "He'll take good care of his sister's kids. But you're right about Shelby. Wrong place, wrong time. It's heartbreaking. She was such a force for good in the community. And Clint...it hurts my heart to think about him."

"Are you two Rutledge and Radcliffe's new in-house investigators?" Blake asked.

Nate and I exchanged a glance.

"We might work cases for them in the future," Nate said. "But we declined their offer to work for them exclusively."

Joe said, "I bet that was a nice offer. They're one of the top defense firms in town. Why'd you turn that down?"

"Well..." I said. "It's complicated. Mostly we like being our own bosses. Fraser Rutledge is a sharp guy, but I wouldn't want him for an employer. Something tells me that would be as stressful as it would be lucrative."

"Merry, call your father in for dinner," Mamma said.

Merry started out the backdoor, then stopped. "What in the—"

"Oh," said Mamma. "That's your father's new pet."

Merry said, "It's—"

"Yes," said Mamma. "I know. A Vietnamese pot-bellied pig. You can thank your sister." She swiveled The Look in my direction. I knew then if not for a near-death experience, at least in Mamma's eyes, I would've already been skinned alive.

Merry and Heather commenced with a chorus of "Oh, how darling," and all such as that. They hurried out the back door.

"Oh no. Mamma, I'm so sorry," I said. "Where—"

"Your father went out Thursday night with Zeke Lyerly and that crowd. To play poker. He's been captivated by the idea of a pig ever since you told him last Sunday about the one you saw. He apparently mentioned this to Zeke."

"And Zeke gave Daddy a pig?" I moved to the window.

"As I understand it, Zeke knew someone who had a pot-bellied pig who had recently given birth to piglets. Through some strange transaction, your father won the pig in the poker game. The piglets had been weaned and spoken for."

"Kinky," Daddy's voice carried into the kitchen.

"What's he calling it?" I scrunched up my face.

"Kinky," said Mamma. "Kinky LeCoeur. That's what your father and Zeke were drinking at the time."

"What does Chumley think about the pig?" I asked.

"He's nearly as enthusiastic as I am," said Mamma.

"Poor Chumley," I said.

Mamma looked at me like I'd lost my mind.

I moved to hug her. "Poor Mamma."

She hugged me tight one more time for good measure. Then she said, "Just remember, if your daddy aggravates me to a stroke, one of you girls is going to have to take care of him. Your sister could well be in Patagonia or some other exotic locale. And your daddy comes with a Basset Hound and a pig."

Susan M. Boyer

Susan M. Boyer is the author of the *USA Today* bestselling Liz Talbot mystery series. Her debut novel, *Lowcountry Boil*, won the Agatha Award for Best First Novel, the Daphne du Maurier Award for Excellence in Mystery/Suspense, and garnered several other award nominations, including the Macavity. The third in the series, *Lowcountry Boneyard*, was a Southern Independent Booksellers Alliance (SIBA) Okra Pick, a Daphne du Maurier Award finalist, and short-listed for the Pat Conroy Beach Music Mystery Prize. Susan loves beaches, Southern food, and small towns where everyone knows everyone, and everyone has crazy relatives. You'll find all of the above in her novels. She lives in Greenville, SC, with her husband and an inordinate number of houseplants.

**The Liz Talbot Mystery Series**
**By Susan M. Boyer**

LOWCOUNTRY BOIL (#1)
LOWCOUNTRY BOMBSHELL (#2)
LOWCOUNTRY BONEYARD (#3)
LOWCOUNTRY BORDELLO (#4)
LOWCOUNTRY BOOK CLUB (#5)

Available at booksellers nationwide and online

Visit www.henerypress.com for details

## Henery Press Mystery Books

And finally, before you go...
Here are a few other mysteries
you might enjoy:

# BOARD STIFF
### Kendel Lynn

## An Elliott Lisbon Mystery (#1)

As director of the Ballantyne Foundation on Sea Pine Island, SC, Elliott Lisbon scratches her detective itch by performing discreet inquiries for Foundation donors. Usually nothing more serious than retrieving a pilfered Pomeranian. Until Jane Hatting, Ballantyne board chair, is accused of murder. The Ballantyne's reputation tanks, Jane's headed to a jail cell, and Elliott's sexy ex is the new lieutenant in town.

Armed with moxie and her Mini Coop, Elliott uncovers a trail of blackmail schemes, gambling debts, illicit affairs, and investment scams. But the deeper she digs to clear Jane's name, the guiltier Jane looks. The closer she gets to the truth, the more treacherous her investigation becomes. With victims piling up faster than shells at a clambake, Elliott realizes she's next on the killer's list.

Available at booksellers nationwide and online

Visit www.henerypress.com for details

# PILLOW STALK

Diane Vallere

## A Madison Night Mystery (#1)

Interior Decorator Madison Night might look like a throwback to the sixties, but as business owner and landlord, she proves that independent women can have it all. But when a killer targets women dressed in her signature style—estate sale vintage to play up her resemblance to fave actress Doris Day—what makes her unique might make her dead.

The local detective connects the new crime to a twenty-year old cold case, and Madison's long-trusted contractor emerges as the leading suspect. As the body count piles up, Madison uncovers a Soviet spy, a campaign to destroy all Doris Day movies, and six minutes of film that will change her life forever.

Available at booksellers nationwide and online

Visit www.henerypress.com for details

# DOUBLE WHAMMY

## Gretchen Archer

### A Davis Way Crime Caper (#1)

Davis Way thinks she's hit the jackpot when she lands a job as the fifth wheel on an elite security team at the fabulous Bellissimo Resort and Casino in Biloxi, Mississippi. But once there, she runs straight into her ex-ex husband, a rigged slot machine, her evil twin, and a trail of dead bodies. Davis learns the truth and it does not set her free—in fact, it lands her in the pokey.

Buried under a mistaken identity, unable to seek help from her family, her hot streak runs cold until her landlord Bradley Cole steps in. Make that her landlord, lawyer, and love interest. With his help, Davis must win this high stakes game before her luck runs out.

Available at booksellers nationwide and online

Visit www.henerypress.com for details

# THE DEEP END

Julie Mulhern

## The Country Club Murders (#1)

Swimming into the lifeless body of her husband's mistress tends to ruin a woman's day, but becoming a murder suspect can ruin her whole life.

It's 1974 and Ellison Russell's life revolves around her daughter and her art. She's long since stopped caring about her cheating husband, Henry, and the women with whom he entertains himself. That is, until she becomes a suspect in Madeline Harper's death. The murder forces Ellison to confront her husband's proclivities and his crimes—kinky sex, petty cruelties and blackmail.

As the body count approaches par on the seventh hole, Ellison knows she has to catch a killer. But with an interfering mother, an adoring father, a teenage daughter, and a cadre of well-meaning friends demanding her attention, can Ellison find the killer before he finds her?

Available at booksellers nationwide and online

Visit www.henerypress.com for details

# MURDER IN G MAJOR

Alexia Gordon

## A Gethsemane Brown Mystery (#1)

With few other options, African-American classical musician Gethsemane Brown accepts a less-than-ideal position turning a group of rowdy schoolboys into an award-winning orchestra. Stranded without luggage or money in the Irish countryside, she figures any job is better than none. The perk? Housesitting a lovely cliffside cottage. The catch? The ghost of the cottage's murdered owner haunts the place. Falsely accused of killing his wife (and himself), he begs Gethsemane to clear his name so he can rest in peace.

Gethsemane's reluctant investigation provokes a dormant killer and she soon finds herself in grave danger. As Gethsemane races to prevent a deadly encore, will she uncover the truth or star in her own farewell performance?

Available at booksellers nationwide and online

Visit www.henerypress.com for details

CPSIA information can be obtained
at www.ICGtesting.com
Printed in the USA
LVOW01s2120040716

495098LV00011B/125/P